MILKSHAKE UP

CRIME À LA MODE, BOOK 2

CHRISTY BARRITT

CHAPTER ONE

SERENA LAVINIA CRANKED up the volume on the music screaming through her speakers as she turned around in a driveway and headed back down Seagull Lane.

She and her ice cream truck, Elsa, had a standing date with one of the residents on the street.

Arnie Blankenship.

But today, he'd stood her up. There had to be a misunderstanding. It was the only explanation she could think of.

"You scream, I scream, we all scream for ice cream!" she yelled out the window as the salty, humid air floated inside. The sound of seagulls squawking mixed with her voice and the electronic strands of "Are You Sleeping?"

She'd decided to try out a different sales pitch every day. Her current slogan of the day was one of her favorites.

Arnie, her newest favorite customer, knew that Serena drove Elsa past his vacation house every day between 11:30 and 12:00 p.m. And, every day, he came out and bought an average of ten different treats from her. He didn't even get the same kind each time. Instead, he liked variety. Firecrackers, push-up pops, chocolate chip cookie sandwiches, snow cones, lemon ice. Lately, he'd even splurged and gotten milkshakes from the new soft-serve machine she'd just had installed.

Today, Arnie hadn't come out. The sweltering late-June day screamed that it needed some ice cream to cure its hot, temperamental problems. Certainly Arnie would agree.

Serena looked over at her dog, Scoops, who sat in the seat beside her. "What do you think, boy? Is this obnoxious that I'm going past his house twice?"

The dog barked at her and wagged his tail.

Scoops didn't care what Serena did as long as he occasionally got an orange Creamsicle as a reward for all his hard work. One might think that a dog couldn't do hard work in the ice cream truck business, but Scoops was one of her main attractions.

Kids *loved* the dog. And they *loved* ice cream. So when they saw an ice cream truck with a dog's head hanging out the window?

It was a win-win for everybody involved, she'd say.

Serena slowed as she passed Arnie's house again. The man lived in a two-story home with dark-blue wood siding and neat white trim.

His car sat in the driveway, signifying he hadn't gone anywhere. Serena assumed he hadn't walked to the ocean since Arnie had told her he wasn't the beach type. Instead, he liked to walk the shoreline early in the morning and late at night when it wasn't too hot.

It didn't matter to Serena either way.

Mostly what Serena cared about was making sure her business stayed profitable. Maybe it was her Evil Queen outfit that was scaring people off today.

She didn't usually go the dark route, but she'd just watched *Snow White* and had felt inspired. Every day she dressed as a different character or personality, just to keep life interesting. She already had the medieval dress, so she'd just had to add the cape and crown.

"You scream, I scream, we all scream for," she raised her voice, "ice cream!"

No one came out.

"Maybe he decided to go to the beach after all," she muttered to Scoops. "Oh well. It was worth a shot."

A sand dune bordering the beach marked the end of the lane. Once again, Serena turned around.

This was it. She wouldn't push any more, even though her nature was to do exactly that.

But as she glanced up at Arnie's house one last time, she noticed from this angle that his door was cracked open.

"Why would he leave his door open?" she muttered to Scoops.

Her dog barked.

That was strange. The man was particular. Maybe he didn't even realize he'd left his door ajar.

Either way, Arnie was practically inviting somebody to come in and steal his things.

"That settles it," Serena told Scoops. "I'll be a Good Samaritan and let my new favorite customer know that his door is open. No hidden agendas. No lurking sales pitches. I'm just being neighborly."

The little terrier wagged his tail in agreement, his ears perked.

Serena pulled into Arnie's driveway and put her

truck in Park. As she climbed out, she patted her leg, motioning for Scoops to follow. "Come on, boy."

Scoops jumped out and trailed beside her as she walked up the wooden stairs leading to the front door of the beachside home.

She knocked before leaning inside and calling, "Hello?"

There was no response.

"Maybe Arnie left in a hurry and the wind pushed the door open," she told Scoops. "It could happen."

Scoops let out a little whine beside her and stared up, as if trying to tell her something.

Serena tried to interpret the sound. "What is it, boy?"

Scoops made the same noise again. What was his doggy sense telling him?

She glanced through the front door again. She'd never seen the inside of Arnie's house before. The man had always met Serena on the street when he came out to make his daily purchases.

The interior appeared to be updated with new furnishings and turquoise accents.

Her gaze caught on something in the distance.

That almost looked like a . . . a hand stretched

across the kitchen table in the distance. She could see only part of the area because the wall jutted out.

"If he's sitting at the table, why isn't he answering me when I called?" she muttered aloud.

If he wanted to pretend not to be home, wouldn't he at least withdraw his arm so he wouldn't be seen?

Scoops made the same whiny sound beside her.

"Something's wrong, isn't it?" Serena frowned and adjusted the crown on top of her head. She stepped inside the house and called, "Hello?"

Still no response, nor did the arm move.

A bad feeling snaked up her spine. Something was wrong—like green bean-flavored popsicle wrong.

Slowly, Serena stepped forward, her body hunched with trepidation. Scoops remained beside her. Her throat tightened as she anticipated what she might find.

More of the table came into view.

That was definitely an arm.

And was that . . . a head resting against it?

Her lungs froze.

It almost looked like someone had passed out at the table.

Was that Arnie Blankenship? Had he had some type of medical episode?

She took a few more steps and gasped as the scene fully came into view.

That was definitely Arnie.

And he was definitely sprawled out on the table.

Serena studied him. His chest didn't appear to be rising and falling. And his skin looked sickly pale.

Was he . . . dead?

Her heart lodged in her throat as she continued to study him.

Why in the world were there uncountable ice cream wrappers laid out on the table around him? She'd have to figure that out later.

Right now, she grabbed her phone and called 911.

"TELL me again how you managed to find another dead body." Police Chief Cassidy Chambers leveled her gaze at Serena as they stood in Arnie Blankenship's living room.

Serena shifted, feeling uncomfortable under the chief's scrutiny.

She knew how this looked. Suspicious. Way too suspicious.

Just last week, Serena had found a body in a

swimming pool. How was it possible to find two dead people within two weeks?

"He was a regular customer, so I got worried when he didn't come out to buy anything today," Serena explained.

Cassidy glanced back at the man's body as the medical examiner leaned over him. Another officer searched the rest of the house for any evidence of what might have happened. Serena had looked— just a little—before Cassidy had arrived. She hadn't noticed anything amiss.

"When you say this guy was a regular customer, you really mean he was a regular customer, don't you?" Cassidy raised an eyebrow before looking back at the wrappers on the table.

Serena nodded, a mental montage playing, complete with music, as she remembered their daily ice cream encounters. "He bought stuff every day. He was a *very* good customer, and he really loved ice cream. Do you think he died of natural causes?"

Her throat burned as she waited for Cassidy's response. In her gut, Serena knew there was nothing natural about this. She didn't have to be Sherlock Cones—as her aunt jokingly called her—to figure this out.

"It's too early to tell. I'll have to let Doc Clemson

be the judge of that. I'm sure he'll run a tox screen. The man can't be much older than thirty, and he appears to be in good health, other than being a little overweight."

Serena folded her arms over her chest, unable to get the image out of her mind. Despite that, she glanced back at Arnie one more time. Much of the ice cream around him had melted, some of it seeping from the wrappers and puddling on the kitchen table.

It seemed surreal that this had happened.

"What did you touch when you got inside?" Cassidy studied Serena's face. "Anything?"

Serena shrugged as she replayed her entry. "Nothing. The door was open, so I didn't touch it. I called hello. When Arnie didn't answer, I looked inside. That's when I saw someone at the table."

Cassidy frowned. "If you remember anything else, please let me know."

"Of course."

Just then, Clemson—the medical examiner and island doctor—called Cassidy over to look at something. As Cassidy walked away, Serena glanced down at the desk beside her.

A computer and well-used calculator sat there. But those weren't what caught her eye.

She saw the name Rippled across the top of some letterhead stationery. She didn't have time to read all the text, but she pulled out a few key phrases, including the words "terminated," "severance," and "confidentiality agreement."

Had Arnie been fired from his job? Maybe that would explain what he was doing down here for so long. Later, Serena would do some research on the company. She'd never heard of it before, but now she was more curious than ever.

Another paper beneath that one had the words "Patent Application" at the top.

She looked up just in time to hear Clemson say, "It could be a heart attack or some other medical emergency. But his face is swollen, and there are hives on the side of his neck. Those can be classic signs of poisoning."

Serena gasped. Had Arnie been poisoned?

She glanced down at her outfit.

The Evil Queen.

The one who'd poisoned Snow White.

What if they thought . . . ?

Heat climbed up her neck.

Cassidy glanced over at Serena, a knot forming between her eyes. She'd obviously heard Serena gasp.

She might even think Serena looked guilty.

Because Serena undoubtedly *did* look guilty.

Serena pointed behind her at the door and began creeping that way, Scoops scooting along beside her. "I should go . . ."

Cassidy's eyes narrowed. "Serena, I'm going to need you to pretend you didn't hear that."

"Of course." She nodded, probably too adamantly.

"Until we know if this man was poisoned, I need to ask you to suspend your ice cream sales."

Serena clutched her heart. "I can assure you I did not poison his apple. I mean, ice cream."

Cassidy's face remained placid. "I mean it, Serena. Don't sell any more ice cream until we have some answers, and stay on the island in case we need to talk, okay?"

Serena suddenly felt lightheaded, but she nodded. "I've got nowhere to go. I'll be here. Doing my thing. Not selling ice cream. Not selling ice cream that's poisoned."

Cassidy tilted her head, scrutinizing Serena with her gaze. "You don't know anything about this, do you, Serena?"

"Of course not."

"Good."

But a new sense of worry filled Serena. What if one of her treats had somehow ended up killing a man?

And the even bigger question: was the rest of her ice cream safe?

CHAPTER TWO

AS SERENA STEPPED OUTSIDE, she saw several people standing on the street, staring at the two police vehicles in front of Arnie's house. No doubt they were curious about what was going on inside.

Serena recognized two of the people gawking there as past patrons of her ice cream truck. She had the perfect job for mingling with tourists on the island. That fact was normally something she loved.

Right now, she felt in mourning for her best customer.

Serena and Scoops walked back toward her truck. As they did, she straightened her crown and reminded herself that she hadn't done anything wrong.

So why did she feel guilty?

Arnie's image kept slamming back into her mind as "Summertime Blues" played on her mental soundtrack.

"Is everything okay in there?" A forty-something brunette stepped toward Serena before tightly crossing her arms over her chest. Her lips were pursed with worry, and white circles edged her eyes —sunglass lines. Nothing made a person look like a reverse raccoon more quickly. Serena had seen it plenty of times before.

"I'm probably not allowed to say." Serena paused near the woman, and Scoops sat at her feet.

"That means he's dead, doesn't it? If it wasn't something serious then you would be able to say."

"I don't want to get myself in trouble." Serena was probably already in enough hot water as it was. She didn't want to do anything to make Cassidy give her more attention.

She adjusted her crown again, wishing she'd picked any other costume to wear today.

The woman shook her head, running a hand over her face. "I can't believe that. Arnie just seemed like the nicest guy. We talked whenever we ran into each other. My husband and I had even mentioned having him over for dinner sometime."

"I agree that he was a nice guy," the man beside her said.

The man was probably in his early thirties and had blue hair that was short on the sides and long on top. The color reminded Serena of the Blue Raspberry slushies she'd had as a child. Despite the hair, something about him made her think of a hipster. Maybe it was his tiny shorts or tight T-shirt or the socks that came to his knees.

"I ran into him every morning when I was walking on the beach," Blue Raspberry continued. "Seemed like a real smart guy. A computer genius, from what I understood."

"Is that what he did for a living?" Serena asked, remembering Arnie's desk. "Something with technology?"

She tried to put the pieces together in her head. She might need to clear her own name. The more knowledge she was armed with, the more equipped she would be for the fight—a fight for good versus evil, she mentally said in her best dramatic narrator voice.

However, right now, she was dressed like she was on the dark side.

"He did something with some kind of company." The man brushed his mop of hair from his eyes. "He worked on the app for them, if I understood him correctly."

"He seemed like the kind who might like computers," Serena said. Arnie had been a little pasty, a little nerdy, and he laughed at his own jokes a lot.

"What happened to him?" The brunette lowered her voice and stared at Serena, as if she fully expected an answer now that they'd developed rapport.

"Like I said, I'm not allowed to say." Serena shrugged. "But it's not good."

The woman pressed her fingers against her temples while the man stood idly by, not making any move to comfort her.

The two of them must be strangers. They gave off that vibe.

"Did you see anything suspicious happening at the house?" Serena might as well get some information while they were chatting, right? She never knew when that might come in handy.

Blue Raspberry shook his head. "Nah, man. I didn't see anything. The guy kept pretty much to himself. If I didn't run into him on the beach, I wouldn't have even known he was staying there."

"Same here," the woman said. "Except I ran into

him at the beach at night. My family's been having a bonfire there every evening. Two nights ago, we invited him to join us, but he said he had too much work to do."

"Did either of you ever see anybody else at his house?" Serena continued, watching from the corner of her eye as Scoops chased a butterfly.

"I can't say that I did." The woman's eyes widened as soon as the words left her lips. "No, I take that back. There was a red sedan sitting there last night."

She had Serena's interest now. "What do you mean by red sedan? When?"

"It was late. I couldn't sleep, and I didn't want to wake my husband up, so I went and sat on the deck for a little while. The weather was so lovely and cool and . . . well, I guess that's not really what you want to hear." The woman frowned.

"You're doing great," Serena said, desperately wanting to hear more.

"Anyway, it was past midnight when I came outside," the woman continued, wringing her hands. "There was a car in the driveway. About ten minutes after I went outside, I saw a man leave the house and climb into the vehicle. He pulled away, and that was that."

Could this woman have seen the killer? Serena's pulse raced. "Could you identify the man if you saw him again?"

"No." The woman frowned. "It was way too dark. I'm fairly certain it was a man, based on the height and the build."

"What about the car? Any idea what it looked like?"

"Like I said, it was red. Two doors. Had a dent in the back bumper."

"How about the plates? Were they local?" Serena's reporter's instincts emerged before she could stop them. Not that she would want to stop them. She needed answers right now.

"I'm sorry." The woman fanned her face, as if she were getting hot. "But I really wasn't paying that much attention. I'm not sure I could've seen them anyway."

"No, that's great. Thanks for your help. You're probably going to need to tell the police that also in a few minutes." As Serena said the words, she glanced back and saw Cassidy strut from the house. The police chief's eyes narrowed as she saw Serena talking to the neighbors.

Serena smiled at her, pretending she didn't know she may have just messed up part of Cassidy's investigation. She was sure Cassidy wanted to be the first person to talk to any potential witnesses. But Serena hadn't looked for witnesses to talk to. They'd just landed in her lap, so what could she say?

She climbed back into her ice cream truck before Cassidy could scold her. It looked like her route was over for today.

Serena felt a headache coming on. Things never quite worked out the way she thought they should. But she had a feeling things might get worse before they got better.

———

SERENA COULDN'T BRING herself to go back to her house and sit by herself. Instead, she pulled up to the house of the island's newspaper editor, Ernestine Sanders. Well, actually Ernestine was no longer a newspaper editor, but her nephew, Webster Newsome, was. Serena still hadn't accepted that fact.

She supposed that Webster was an okay enough guy, but Serena felt like she should rightfully take the position as editor of the newspaper. Webster still didn't know the island that well, and, even though he came with gobs of experience, that shouldn't matter in these cases.

Serena was supposed to meet him in a couple hours so they could go over their stories for this week. But, in the meantime, she wanted to get a good look at her inventory. If someone had messed with her ice cream, then they'd messed with her.

She turned her truck off and climbed into the back. Opening the freezer, she pulled out an ice cream sandwich. Carefully, she examined the wrapper for any signs it had been tampered with.

She saw nothing.

A knock sounded, and she nearly jumped out of her skin. Webster's face appeared through the glass.

She pulled the latch, and he climbed inside. As he did, the scent of newspaper ink—he read the *Washington Post* every morning—and leather floated with him.

The man was average build and size. Though he'd been here for a week now, he still hadn't adapted to a beach style of loose, lightweight clothing. Instead, he liked jeans and polo shirts. He also had plastic-framed glasses and short brown hair with a side part.

"Serena? What are you doing here so early?" He pushed his glasses up and frowned. "And your outfit today . . . it's interesting."

This outfit might be one of her biggest regrets. "It's a long story."

"I have time." Webster crossed his arms and looked at the ice cream in her hands as he hunched due to the low ceiling.

She briefly considered giving him the ice cream sandwich and telling him to try it, to test out her theory that it might be poisoned. But then she really might be guilty of killing someone.

And Serena didn't actually wish anything bad to happen to the man.

"A man died, and he was surrounded by my ice cream treats, and now I'm worried that someone did something to my stock." The words came out fast and almost reckless.

"What?" Webster stared at her, confusion etched into the lines at the corners of his eyes.

Serena slowed her words and told him everything that happened at Arnie's. As Webster listened, he leaned against a freezer, nodding at all the appropriate times. He was a decent listener. She had to give him that.

"What is it with you finding dead bodies lately?" he asked. "Is this normal?"

"That's a great question. I have no idea. It's becoming a hobby, it seems." The ice cream sandwich in her hands began to melt and drip onto the floor. As it did, she felt her eyes tear up. Quickly, she pulled herself together. "There's no use crying over . . . melted ice cream, right?"

He leveled his gaze. "Maybe you should let the police examine the ice cream, just in case there's evidence left on any of them."

Serena dropped the treat in her hand. What if she'd just contaminated fingerprints that could have been left there? Guilt flooded her.

"Of course," she muttered. "You're right."

For that matter, maybe she should go back to all of her customers and make sure they were okay. But most of them had eaten their ice cream treats right on the spot. They'd seemed okay as she looked at them in her rearview mirror.

Panic froze her.

What if this *was* her fault and other people had died besides Arnie?

Serena's head began to spin as the thought hit her. She pulled off her stupid crown. Had she inadvertently put a curse on this whole truck?

It felt like it.

"Maybe you should sit down." Webster's eyes narrowed with concern.

Serena didn't have to be told twice. She didn't

even bother to go back to the driver's seat. Instead, she lowered herself to the floor.

Scoops climbed into her lap and licked her face. She rubbed the dog's head, finding comfort in her furry friend. It was like the dog could read her mind.

"What should I do?" Serena looked up at Webster, truly at a loss.

"Maybe you should call Chief Chambers and see what she thinks."

"That's a great idea. Except I don't know if I can." Her throat tightened at the thought of talking to Cassidy again.

"What do you mean?" Webster leaned toward her, curiosity—and confusion—in his gaze.

"I don't know. I just feel like the wrong words are going to come out. Like I'll start talking about poisoned apples again or something. And, if any of this is somehow connected to me or if it's my fault . . ." Her voice trailed. She couldn't finish that thought.

"How about this?" Webster placed his hand on her arm. "I'll call her for you."

She looked up at him, surprised by how calm he made her feel. "You'd do that for me?"

"Of course, I would."

Something about Webster's words made Serena feel like he was on her side. She was grateful for that

—even though she still wasn't sure she could trust the man. At least not professionally.

The next moment, Webster dialed Cassidy's number. He spoke with her a few minutes before ending the call and putting his phone back into his pocket.

"The police chief hasn't had any calls about anyone being sick, so you're probably okay," Webster said. "She said not to touch any more of your ice cream, and she would check them out later. Feel better?"

"I feel better that nobody else is sick yet. I don't feel good knowing that this man's death may be coming back to me."

"On the bright side, it looks like we have a new story to cover." Webster offered a feeble smile.

"We?"

"The fact is, you can't cover a story that you might be involved with." Webster pushed his glasses up higher.

Serena crossed her arms, not liking the sound of that. "That's not fair. Before you came here, I was doing all of the stories myself."

"Then don't look at it as an intrusion. Look at it as assistance. Now we can work together."

Serena narrowed her eyes. Webster was spinning

this like it was a good thing, but she wasn't so sure. "And how would you say we should work together?"

"You said you saw the name of this man's company, right?"

"That's right."

He nodded toward Ernestine's house across the lawn. "What do you say we go into the office and see what we can find out about it?"

CHAPTER THREE

A FEW MINUTES LATER, Serena, Webster, Scoops, and Ernestine all sat around an old computer with a monitor big enough to microwave a watermelon.

Not that people did that.

But still.

Ernestine insisted the PC still worked perfectly fine and they should use it to investigate Arnie's business.

Webster typed in the word Rippled, and they waited until the results populated the screen. Unfortunately, whereas on a new computer it would take two seconds, on Ernestine's outdated technology, it took almost five minutes. It was a wonder the online paper ever got published with this beast.

"You really need to update this, Aunt Ernestine." Webster tapped his foot.

"It runs fine," she said.

Ernestine took a sip of her green smoothie, something she attributed her youthful figure to. She'd utilized her smoothie protocol long before the fruity drinks were cool.

"Do you know what the problem is with today's younger generation?" Ernestine continued. "They're so wasteful. Something breaks, and they get a new one. I believe in using things for as long as I can. It's responsible."

"Aunt Ernestine—" Webster started.

"It's true. You guys are always preaching about not being wasteful, about the importance of recycling. Seems like it only applies to plastic bags and bottles, though. Electronics are a free-for-all. Don't get me started on clothes and water."

Webster frowned. "Point noted."

No one dared say anything else. Certainly not Serena. No way did she want a lecture right now.

The computer dinged, and Webster scanned the results, clicking on one. A few minutes later, the website loaded. Serena rubbed Scoops's head as she waited, anticipation growing inside her.

"Okay, look at this." Webster pointed to the

screen. "Rippled is a new fitness app. It prides itself in being different because, not only can you record what you eat and keep track of the calories that way, but it also gives you customized food and fitness plans, plus video chat support."

"Sounds like a good idea," Serena said. "Not a hundred percent original but okay. It's kind of a weird name, though."

"How much do you want to bet Ripped was already taken?" Webster cast a glance at her.

"Could be. But I think their name could be their first downfall."

"When I click on the 'About' section, it gives me a little history of the company. It looks like it was started three years ago by three men. One of those men just happens to be our dead guy."

Serena stared at the screen. Sure enough, there was Arnie Blankenship. He looked so happy in the photo as he smiled at the screen.

However, as Serena looked at the rest of the pictures, she realized that one of the three was not like the other two. Her dead guy stood out like a sore thumb in the row of pictures.

Whereas Arnie hadn't been necessarily over-weight, he definitely hadn't been in shape. He'd had the beginnings of a double chin and arms without definition and a haircut that made his face look rounder than necessary.

The other two guys looked like they lived to exercise. Their skin was tan and their muscles bulky. They wore sleeveless shirts, and their smiles seemed self-assured, maybe even cocky.

"It appears that our dead guy was in charge of finance and technology," Webster said. "And what I'm taking that to mean is that he funded and developed most of the operations for this startup."

"He seems like a finance and tech kind of guy." Serena remembered seeing the computer and calculator on his desk.

"The other man . . . is a self-proclaimed fitness guru." Webster leaned closer to the screen. "And then the third guy is a dietician."

"That still doesn't tell us why Arnie might have died," Serena said.

"No, it doesn't. But let's look at some of these other links. Maybe one of them will have an answer."

Serena could only hope.

AN HOUR LATER, Webster, Ernestine, and Serena

had discovered that Rippled was in serious financial trouble. The company had started a Kickstarter campaign to help raise money. They'd also had to lay off about half of their workforce. There had only been about fifty people in the company anyway, but more than twenty had been let go.

What if Arnie had been under a lot of stress and had decided to end his own life? She didn't like to think about it, but she knew that could be reality at times. The man could have overdosed on something. That might present like a poison, right?

Something about that theory didn't fit her overall image of Arnie, though. He'd seemed so happy. Nothing about him screamed that he was stressed or depressed.

Which then brought her around to yet another theory.

If the company was in trouble, maybe there was friction between the founders. Could one of them have followed Arnie here and killed him?

It seemed plausible. But Serena had no idea exactly how she was going to figure that out.

Maybe Webster would have some ideas. But that would mean she would need to ask his opinion.

She fought a frown. Asking for his opinion might make it seem like she was incompetent. Or it could make her seem like she was humble. She wasn't sure which route she wanted to go.

She decided to leave it in Webster's hands instead. She waited for him to speak, rubbing Scoops's head as the seconds ticked past.

"I'm going to see what I can find out about these guys," Webster said. "It appears that this company is based out of Philadelphia. I'll see if I can find out whether Arnie's two business partners are still up there. Serena, I think you should continue to talk to neighbors and see if there was anybody else coming and going from Arnie's place over the past few days. Do you think you can handle that?"

"Absolutely," she said.

"Great. Then we'll reconnect tomorrow morning. For breakfast?"

That appeared to be Webster's favorite time and place to connect. And Serena didn't mind. It was nice to have someone to hang out with, especially considering that most of the people around her had found the loves of their lives and she often felt like a third wheel.

"Sounds good," she said. "I'll see you at 8:00 a.m. tomorrow at our normal place?"

Webster smiled. "Great. I will see you then."

CHAPTER FOUR

SERENA'S THOUGHTS were still racing as she pulled up to the camper she called home. Hers was one of many located on Pamlico Sound, where residents could see amazing sunsets. Most of the RVs here were permanent. Many had little decks near the front door, and some even had landscaping set up.

She parked her ice cream truck in front of the camper as she always did. Then she and Scoops stomped toward the front door. Well, she stomped and Scoops trotted. He was too cute to stomp.

Serena only went inside long enough to change out of her Evil Witch outfit and into some comfy shorts and a T-shirt. After feeding and watering Scoops, she wandered back outside, leaving the door open so her dog could come and go as he pleased.

Even though it was a hot day, she lay on her hammock for a minute to think, pondering what had happened to Arnie and how to handle things.

Even more so, Serena couldn't stop thinking about if she could somehow be involved.

Not that she was involved on purpose.

That's why it didn't surprise her when she saw Cassidy pull up in her law enforcement vehicle ten minutes later.

Chief Chambers climbed out, still wearing her police uniform, and strode toward Serena and Scoops. "How are you doing, Serena?"

"I've been better," Serena said. There was no need to beat around the bush.

"I need to check out some of your ice cream," Cassidy said. "Is that a problem?"

"Help yourself," Serena said. "I have nothing to hide."

Serena walked over and opened the back of the vehicle for her. Cassidy hesitated before climbing inside.

"This brings back memories," she said.

"You were the original crime-solving ice cream lady," Serena reminded her. Cassidy had owned Elsa before she became police chief. The career had never quite fit her, though. She had a natural propensity for solving crimes.

"I guess I was." Cassidy turned toward her. "That doesn't mean you should take my place in that role. These crimes can be serious. I would hate to see you get hurt, and, unfortunately, that's what can happen sometimes."

Serena nodded. "I know. I didn't ask to be involved in this, and, whether I had found Arnie's dead body or not, the ice cream at the scene would have led to me being mixed up in this one way or another."

Cassidy frowned. "I know. And I'm sorry. I know this can't be easy for you."

Scoops barked, almost as if he understood what was being said.

Without saying anything else, Cassidy climbed into the vehicle. She pulled on some gloves as she began surveying the back where the ice cream was located.

Serena stayed outside and picked up Scoops as she watched Cassidy begin to take pictures of everything.

This was serious. Serena knew without a doubt that this investigation had the power to change the trajectory of her future. Her stomach clenched at the thought.

After Cassidy finished taking pictures, she put her phone back into her pocket, opened a freezer, and picked up a fudge pop. She examined it with a flashlight before lowering it again, picking up something else, and going through the same process. This continued for at least fifteen of the various treats.

What was she looking for? And the even greater question, had she found it?

Finally, Cassidy placed each of those treats into plastic bags and stepped from the back of the truck. "I'm going to need to take these with me."

"You think they've been tainted?" Serena could hardly breathe as she waited for Cassidy's response.

"I can't be sure. We're going to need to send them to the lab."

"Why do I have a feeling there's something you're not saying?" Cassidy knew something, didn't she? What had she discovered?

Cassidy frowned before pulling a treat out and showing it to her. "I can't be sure, Serena, but it almost looks like a prick mark on some of these wrappers."

Serena leaned closer, desperate to understand what Cassidy was talking about. She saw nothing.

"Where?"

"Right there." Cassidy pointed to an area on the wrapper.

As Serena squinted, she saw it. The mark was barely visible to the human eye, but it was there. A tiny, tiny hole.

Just big enough for something like a needle to fit through.

A needle that could inject poison into her products.

Her stomach clenched.

This wasn't good. It wasn't good at all.

If only a kiss from a handsome prince would solve all her problems. But that was wishful thinking. And there were no handsome princes around anyway.

SERENA'S BUSINESS had officially been shut down. For now, at least.

She had thrown the rest of her stock away, knowing she couldn't take a chance on selling it to anybody.

She didn't even make it back to her hammock to feel sorry for herself. Instead, she and Scoops sat on her steps. Serena rested her chin in her hands as she contemplated everything that happened, a distinct feeling of doom washing over her.

"Serena," someone said.

Serena looked up and saw her friend Kai standing there. Kai was in her forties, but she wore her blonde hair back in tiny braids. All the sunbathing she had done throughout the years made her skin look more wrinkled and leathery than it probably should at her age.

But the woman had proven herself to be a good friend, so Serena couldn't complain—not that she would anyway. After all the ways Serena dressed, who was she to judge anyone else?

Scoops jumped up and ran toward Kai. He was rewarded with a big pat on the head.

"What's going on?" Kai sat down beside Serena and handed her some canned homemade pickles. "And, by the way, I made these for you. I started to bring them by earlier, but I saw the police chief here."

Kai loved canning and basically anything that had to do with living a homestead type of life here on the island. She worked part time for Serena's Aunt Skye.

Serena gave her the update on what had

happened today, and Kai listened to each new detail. "Man, that's rough. Sorry. If your ice cream really was poisoned, who would have done that? Who had access to your truck?"

The good news was that Kai hadn't assumed Serena had done it. Serena was thankful for that.

"I have no idea," Serena said. "I always keep it locked up at night when I'm sleeping."

"How about when you're out on the town? Do you lock it up wherever you go?"

"I try to. I mean, I don't want anything to get stolen."

"Does anybody else have the keys?"

That was a good question. "I suppose Cassidy might have an extra set since she's the one I bought it from. But nobody else."

Kai walked over to the truck and examined the handles. "This wouldn't be too hard to pick."

That was an interesting statement. Serena wondered exactly what Kai had done in her past. It wouldn't surprise her if the woman had been involved in some petty crimes. She had that "rebel without a cause" vibe sometimes.

"Do you think somebody picked my lock just so they could poison my ice cream?" Serena asked.

Kai shrugged as she walked back over to Serena's

deck. "I'm not stating anything. I am just brain-storming ideas. Otherwise, they would have been poisoned somewhere in transit, right? Either at the manufacturer or maybe through the truck driver who brought it over to the island. Where exactly do you get your products from?"

"I order everything wholesale. Then I drive over to Hatteras once a week so I can pick up my new stock."

"You pick it up from the same person every week?"

Serena nodded. "Yes."

"He or she seem trustworthy?"

Serena shrugged. "I suppose. Though I've never really thought about it."

"So, if it didn't happen at the manufacturer, and if the distributor didn't touch it, then that just leaves somebody breaking into your truck. You just have to figure out when that might have happened. If this guy bought the ice cream from you yesterday, and he ate it last night and that's when he died, then it would have needed to happen sometime before that. You said nobody else has gotten sick?"

"That's what Cassidy said."

"Then it looks like you might have a time frame to

work with. But if no one else has gotten sick, then I fail to see how this could go back to your ice cream. I could understand if there were multiple victims maybe."

Serena nodded, her friend's words making sense. "I'm glad you came by, Kai. You've really given me a lot to think about. I appreciate it."

She smiled. "It's no problem. I like to help whenever I can."

As her friend left, Serena remained sitting on her front steps with Scoops. It was already getting late, and the sun was starting to sink in the sky.

As it did, Scoops began growling beside her. "What is it, boy?"

Scoops continued to growl.

Serena scanned everything around her but didn't see anything. Her best guess was maybe it was a bird or a squirrel.

But she didn't see one of those either.

As the hair on her dog's back began to rise, alarm washed through her. What was going on?

She picked up Scoops and began to walk in the direction he'd been barking. The dog's body remained tense, and he continued to growl.

As Serena walked around her ice cream truck, a person dressed in black darted from the camper beside hers. The man dodged between the other RVs in the area, not bothering to look back.

Why had that man been watching her?

She started to run after him, but she realized there was no use. He had too much of a head start.

Instead, she watched as he disappeared into the woods in the distance.

Serena realized the killer most likely knew who she was. She was going to need to find him if she wanted answers—and to clear her name.

CHAPTER FIVE

THE NEXT MORNING, Serena, as per her normal schedule, got dressed and then posted to her social media accounts. She'd gained ten thousand new followers just in the past week. People loved watching her makeup tips. Who would have ever thought she could make a go of it?

I Am Quick Change was becoming an internet phenomenon.

Once she was done posting for the day, she walked with Scoops across the road to the ocean. It was the perfect way to start her day.

With a walk on the beach.

She always tried to go as the sun was rising.

Serena had always been an early riser anyway. In fact, she'd gotten up before six so she could film her

YouTube video and take some photos for her Instagram accounts.

Today, she'd decided to dress like Dorothy from *The Wizard of Oz*. Sometimes that's how she felt. Like she was the girl who'd been dropped into a strange land—a land where she might be accused of murder.

She'd hardly slept all night, thinking about yesterday's events. Her face showed evidence of that this morning. She applied entirely more makeup than usual trying to cover up the circles beneath her eyes.

As her feet pounded the soft sand, her mind tried to sort out her thoughts.

What if it was discovered that her ice cream *had* been poisoned? And, aside from that, when was she going to be cleared to start selling her treats again? Without that money, it was going to be hard to pay her rent.

Granted, her aunt owned the camper where Serena was staying, and Skye might cut her some slack. But she didn't want to be a freeloader. She preferred to make her own way whenever possible. In the summer months, every day counted.

As Serena and Scoops got halfway into their walk, she paused.

There it was. Another piece of art.

She still wasn't sure who the artist was, but every day he or she left a brilliant picture formed entirely from seashells. Today, the artist had left a mermaid for everyone to enjoy. The figure was six feet long and had been arranged far from the water, near the sand dunes.

Serena had been doing articles on each day's new creation, and she'd gotten a lot of positive feedback on her stories. In fact, she'd heard that people were traveling to the island just to see these creations. They were quite the draw.

As the early morning sun pressed on her shoulders and ghost crabs scampered across the sand, Serena stared at the picture. The artist had used purple shells for the tail and greenish ones to cover the chest area. Orange shells comprised the hair.

The creator had nailed it. This just might be one of this artist's best creations yet. The design was stunning.

Serena pulled out her phone and took several pictures of it as Scoops sniffed around on the dunes.

Later, she'd work on adding some text to the photos and then she'd turn it in so the article could run in the evening. The nice part about having an online newspaper was that articles could be published at any time.

She still wasn't used to Webster being the editor, and she missed Ernestine being in charge. Ernestine had mostly let her do whatever she wanted, which was the primary reason why Serena liked her so much.

Webster did have a decent background in journalism, and Serena knew that she could probably learn a lot from the man. But that didn't stop her from feeling slightly resentful that he'd shown up here. Just when Serena thought she was getting over it, the feelings reared again.

She called to Scoops, and they continued down the beach. Finally, they cut across the parking lot and walked toward The Crazy Chefette, her favorite restaurant here on the island. As she walked, she called her Aunt Skye just to check in.

Skye didn't appear to have heard anything about what happened.

Not yet, at least.

As Serena ended the call, she knew it was time to meet Webster and see if he had found out anything.

But she knew one thing for sure. If there was any chance she might be accused of Arnie's murder, then she needed to find the real killer—before she ended up in jail herself.

"GOOD NEWS," Webster said.

He'd already been seated in the restaurant and had ordered for both of them by the time Serena arrived. As normal, she had sneaked Scoops in with her and the dog sat beneath her feet, out of sight.

Although Serena felt certain that the restaurant owner, Lisa Dillinger, knew that the dog was there, Lisa had yet to say anything to her about it. Serena definitely wasn't going to be the one to bring it up, especially since Scoops didn't cause any trouble.

"I would love to hear some good news." Serena took a sip of her coffee and stared at Webster for a minute. Why did he look so tired this morning? Was he not sleeping well since he was staying with his aunt?

"Your last article about the art on the beach? It was picked up by a bigger newspaper in Raleigh and in Norfolk. BuzzFeed also ran it, so it's getting a lot of attention online. Good job."

"Who would have thought?" She'd always assumed her big story would be on one of the crimes committed here on the island. She'd take whatever she could get.

"Are you any closer to figuring out who's been putting the exhibits together?" Webster studied her face as he sipped his coffee.

"I've asked around, but no one has seen anything," Serena said. "The person who's behind this must be working all night in order to get this stuff done. I imagine that can't be too easy either considering how dark it gets out here."

"Well, keep working on it. I think part of the reason people are fascinated is because they don't know who the artist is behind it. It's a mystery—the warm and fuzzy type, instead of the devastatingly gruesome."

"Whoever created it is awfully talented. You should see today's creation."

"Surprise me later when you turn the article in." He took another sip of his coffee. "Any update on your ice cream?"

Serena told him about the prick marks Cassidy had found on some of the wrappers. "I'm anxiously waiting to see what Cassidy finds out from the tox screen."

Webster leaned closer. "I know I shouldn't say

anything, but Clemson stopped by Ernestine's place this morning."

He now had Serena's full attention. "And?"

"While he was at the house, he got a phone call. I was trying not to listen, but it was kind of hard not to. The space isn't that big, after all."

"And?" Serena just knew this had something to do with Arnie.

Webster lowered his voice. "The police have ruled Arnie's death a homicide."

Serena sucked in a breath. She wasn't sure if she was relieved or even more upset. She still needed to process everything.

"How did he die?"

"My impression is that he was poisoned."

"If that's true, then the poison was injectable. And my ice cream really might have been tainted." Serena felt the blood leave her face. "If people think I'm guilty, my whole business could be ruined."

Webster reached across the table and squeezed her hand. "Let's not jump ahead of things."

Serena glanced at the table to where his hand met hers. Webster quickly pulled away. He obviously hadn't meant to touch her.

And Serena had to admit that she didn't feel totally repulsed. Actually, she didn't feel repulsed at all. The gesture had been sweet. Webster was just trying to reach out to her and make her feel better.

As a server came and refilled their coffee, they quieted, waiting until she was gone before picking up where their conversation had left off.

Serena cleared her throat. "I expect a call from Cassidy anytime now."

"What are you going to do in the meantime?"

"I told you about the red car that somebody saw at the scene the night before Arnie was murdered?" Serena reminded Webster. "I am going to look around town and see if I can find it."

"Okay."

"Oh, and someone was watching me from behind my neighbor's camper last night. He took off when I saw him."

A wrinkle formed between his eyes. "That's not good."

"It's not. But at least he didn't try anything." Serena repressed the shudder that wanted to materialize. Nothing had happened. So why did she still feel shaken?

"Reporting it sounds like a great idea. I made a couple calls to Arnie's coworkers up in Philly. I haven't heard back yet, but I am going to follow up today. I'm composing the rough draft of my article on his murder now, and I'll send it to you later so you can see what you want to add."

"Sounds good."

Just then, their breakfast was delivered. The two of them had a rule with each other. When the food came, they stopped talking shop.

But that didn't mean that Serena was going to stop thinking about Arnie's death.

That fact was only confirmed when Blue Raspberry approached their table. Serena could tell by the look in his eyes that he had something important to tell them.

CHAPTER SIX

"THERE'S BEEN something on my mind and I don't know who I need to share it with," the man started, crouching near the table as if he didn't want anyone else to hear.

"What's going on?" Serena lowered her fork, knowing her fried potatoes with pineapple and peppers could wait a few more minutes.

"Yesterday, you were asking if we'd seen anybody over at Arnie's place." The man shifted, his eyes darting from the table back up to Serena and then Webster. "I didn't want to say anything, especially since she was standing there."

"Who was standing there?" Serena asked, hardly able to breathe.

"That brunette woman we were talking to yesterday. I didn't catch her name. But I saw her and her husband arguing with Arnie the night before."

Serena sat up straighter. "Did you?"

The woman had failed to mention that fact.

"Did you happen to hear what they were arguing about?" Webster asked.

"I couldn't make out much of what was being said, but it sounded heated. There was something about finances. The two of them—the brunette and her husband—appear to have a tumultuous relationship."

"Do you have any idea why?" Serena asked.

"I only have assumptions." Blue Raspberry man shifted again, looking even more uncomfortable as he glanced around.

"Just between us, what are those assumptions?" Serena leaned closer.

Blue Raspberry glanced behind him again. "I just wonder if Arnie and the brunette . . . if there was something between them. They seemed to like talking a lot whenever I passed them on the beach. I can't imagine that the woman's husband would like that."

"I didn't see the woman's husband there

yesterday when I was talking to you," Serena said, trying to recall the conversation.

"I don't know where he was." Blue Raspberry shifted yet again. "Do you think I should tell this to the police?"

Serena and Webster exchanged a glance.

"It couldn't hurt," Webster said.

Blue Raspberry nodded. "Thanks for listening. I just really didn't know what to do with this information, and then I saw you in here . . ."

"No, we appreciate you sharing what you learned." Serena studied his face for a minute. "Are you a local around here?"

"No, but I've been here for most of the summer. My grandpa owns a place here. I went through a bad breakup and decided a change of scenery would be good for me. So far, so good."

"I bet." Serena nodded. "If you hear anything else, please let us know."

With a nod, the man left the restaurant.

Serena glanced at Webster. "It looks like we may have our first real suspect."

"It looks like we might."

SERENA DIDN'T WANT to drive her ice cream truck around the island, especially since she could no longer sell ice cream until she was cleared. Her only other means of transportation was riding her bike or walking. It was a hot day to do those things, but it looked like she didn't have any other choice.

Back at her camper, she paused by the ice cream truck and leaned closer. "I'm sorry, Elsa. Soon, we'll be in business again. Until then, you just take a little rest."

She waited, almost as if she expected the truck to talk back to her. Of course, it didn't—not even a tune.

After patting Elsa on the hood, Serena pulled on her helmet, put Scoops in the front basket, and hopped on her bicycle.

The only real clues she had was that red vehicle someone had spotted at Arnie's house on the night before he died and the argument between the brunette and Arnie. She couldn't decide which lead she wanted to pursue first.

Serena decided to ride around the island and look for that vehicle. And if she found it, she would call Cassidy and let her know. Serena also wanted to talk to that brunette again and follow up on what Blue Raspberry had told her.

It was already feeling like a scorcher outside today. No doubt if Serena had her ice cream truck, she would be selling her treats left and right.

She fought a frown.

Scoops seemed to be enjoying the ride. His tongue hung out of his mouth, and he looked around at everybody and everything they passed. He was such a good dog.

Serena was so glad that she'd found him on the side of the road and that the owner had decided Serena could keep him. It was nice to have a companion. Serena hadn't realized how much she liked living with her aunt. Now that Skye had gotten married and moved out, it got awfully quiet at her house.

Just as if she was on her ice cream route, Serena hit each of the streets in town, making a right-hand turn each time. For fun, she sang some of the songs that Elsa would normally play, starting with "Boom, Boom, Ain't It Great to Be Crazy?"

It was personally one of her favorites, and it had nothing to do with the fact that the song kind of fit her entire life.

So far, Serena had been down ten streets and hadn't seen any red cars yet.

But as she got to the eleventh street and turned around, she saw a car go by on the highway ahead.

It was red with only two doors.

Was that the car she'd been looking for? Maybe.

Wasting no more time, she began to pedal harder. As soon as she saw a break in the traffic, she crossed the street, breaking her right-hand-turn only rule.

Serena pedaled furiously. She could barely see the red car up ahead.

But the important thing was that she *could* see it.

She had to find out who was inside.

As she sped down the road, cars behind her honked. She knew she should be riding on the side of the road instead of in the middle of the lane. But there wasn't a wide shoulder, and she didn't want to risk getting hurt.

So everybody behind her was going to have to wait.

She mentally apologized.

She did realize, however, that she probably looked like someone straight out of *The Wizard of Oz* in her Dorothy outfit with the dog in her front basket.

She was pretty sure a couple people had even taken a picture of her.

Serena craned her neck again, looking for the object of her obsession.

What? How was this possible?

The red car was gone.

But where?

The vehicle behind her honked.

Serena knew she should move over and let the other cars pass, but she didn't want to. Instead, she peddled harder and harder and harder, wishing she was more in shape. Wishing it wasn't so hot outside. Trying to be careful because she did have a precious dog in her basket.

She searched for the car one more time, but it was gone.

Defeat pressed in on her.

When the vehicle behind her honked again, she glanced over her shoulder.

At least ten cars followed her, all traveling ten miles an hour or less, if she had to guess.

With a frown, Serena pulled off onto a side street and waited for the parade of cars to pass.

Several drivers made some not-so-nice gestures as they zoomed by.

Serena didn't care. She looked in the distance and frowned.

Had she lost the possible killer?

Just as the thought entered her mind, she saw the car again. It turned down a street in the distance.

If she hurried, she might be able to catch it.

CHAPTER SEVEN

A FEW MINUTES LATER, Serena pulled into a driveway behind the red sedan with the dented bumper. The driver had just opened the front door to a cottage as she pressed on her brakes.

"Wait!" she called, drawing in a deep breath.

The forty-something man paused and turned toward her. "Can I help you?"

"Your car was at Arnie Blankenship's house on the night he was killed." She dragged in another breath, her heart racing.

"Who's Arnie Blankenship?" He stared at her as if she'd lost her mind.

"Don't play dumb." She might be the dumb one here, confronting the man like this.

He dropped his hand from the doorknob and

stepped closer. "I don't know who you are or what you're talking about. I just got back into town this morning."

Wait . . . that didn't make sense. "This car was at the scene of a murder."

"I don't see how that's possible. I've been gone for the past week. I was doing a film shoot, and there were five people around me who can verify that."

"Did anyone else have access to your car?"

He shrugged. "I suppose anyone could. I keep the key under the front mat. I figured no one would want this clunker. You happy now?"

Serena wasn't sure she'd call herself happy. But his alibi should be pretty easy to confirm.

"Sorry to disturb you," she muttered. "Any chance I could get your name so we can use it in a potential newspaper article on the murder?"

The man scowled at her and said nothing.

She supposed that answered her question.

He watched as Serena pulled away.

She'd felt so close to finding answers. But that car appeared to be a red herring.

What was she going to do now?

SINCE SERENA WAS ALREADY out this way, she decided to swing past Arnie Blankenship's house. She didn't want to see the house itself. She mostly wanted to see if Mrs. Brunette was still around.

Serena slowed her bike and glanced around the dead-end street. She hadn't exactly seen where Brunette had come from. But, based on what Blue Raspberry had told her, the woman must live in one of the houses close by.

Serena nibbled on her bottom lip for a moment as she contemplated her options.

"What do you think, Scoops?" She patted her dog's head. "Where do you think the woman lives?"

The dog had a great sniffer. If the dog actually understood English, he would probably be able to take Serena right to the woman's place.

Other than going door to door, Serena didn't know exactly how she would find Mrs. Brunette. Besides, most of the people who were here on vacation were probably at the beach right now. It was the perfect beach day with the blue skies and subtle breeze.

She frowned and contemplated her options. She was already here so it seemed like a shame to leave without doing anything.

She supposed when she'd been talking to Blue

Raspberry this morning, she could have gotten some more information from him. It sounded like he knew exactly where this woman lived.

As if on cue, the door to the house next to Arnie's opened, and six people walked out—two adults and four kids. Serena scanned each of their faces. Was one of them Mrs. Brunette?

She sucked in a breath when she recognized the woman. It was! Something had actually worked in her favor for once.

Now Serena needed an excuse to talk to her.

Almost as if Scoops could read her mind, the dog jumped from the bike basket and began running toward the family.

"Scoops!" Serena yelled.

She dropped her bike and began running after her dog. The whole family paused, and the children stooped down to pet the canine.

Serena reached them and shook her head. "I'm so sorry. He got away from me."

Brunette glanced at her, and her eyes widened with recognition. "Aren't you the Evil Queen?"

"Most people just call me the ice cream lady."

She let out a laugh. "Of course. I just knew I recognized you from somewhere—and your little dog too." Her hand went over her mouth.

Clever—even if it wasn't on purpose.

"So funny that I ran into you," Serena started. "I was actually hoping to ask you a couple questions."

The brunette glanced at her family, a flash of . . . something . . . fluttering through her gaze. "Why don't you guys go on to the beach? I'll be there in just a couple minutes."

Serena glanced at the man Brunette was with. He was probably in his late forties with a receding hairline and dark, unfriendly eyes. He nodded and called for his children to follow him.

As soon as they were all out of earshot, Serena turned to the brunette. "I won't take much of your time."

"What's going on?" The woman rubbed her hands together, almost as if nervous.

"I was hoping you could tell me a little bit more about Arnie." Serena rubbed Scoops's head, the dog putting her mind at ease.

"I've told you everything I know."

"Someone told me that they saw you and your husband arguing with Arnie."

The woman's gaze narrowed. "You are the ice cream lady, right? Not the police."

Serena nodded. "That's correct. I'm not here to make an arrest or to even make accusations, for that matter. I'm just a curious girl. Oh, and I am a reporter also. I should probably mention that."

The brunette frowned. "Yes, my husband and I did have an argument with Arnie on the night before he died."

"Why was that?"

The woman glanced at her family as they disappeared over the dune. "Arnie heard my husband and me arguing. The two of us got heated. Arnie didn't like the sound of it, so he came over here to check on us and make sure that everything was okay."

"And was everything okay?"

The woman nodded. "It was fine. My husband and I are both Italian. We get a little passionate sometimes. We love big and we fight big. Arnie was worried, and we told him that we appreciated his concern, but we were fine. Then he went on his merry way. That's it."

"You were arguing about finances?" Serena continued.

A knot formed between the woman's eyes. "How did you know that?"

"A neighbor overheard."

She shrugged and let out a breath. "I didn't think we were talking about those details quite so loud, but okay. Yes, it was about finances. My husband is an entrepreneur, so we usually live with either feast or famine. It's a fact of life. We don't always see eye to eye about it."

"So nothing else happened?" Serena verified.

"Nothing else happened."

Serena nodded. The woman didn't seem distressed or like she was silently crying out for help. "And you don't know anything else about Arnie's death, right?"

"My husband did say he heard Arnie arguing with someone inside his house on the day before he died," she offered. "He didn't see any faces. Didn't see any cars. He only heard their voices rising."

"Could he make out anything they said?"

"Only something about a cell phone. I'm sorry I can't be more help."

"Good to know. Thanks for your help. And I hope you enjoy the rest of your vacation."

With that said, Serena leaned down and picked up Scoops. Maybe she had more answers now.

Maybe.

What she didn't have was a suspect.

BUT WHEN SERENA got back to her camper and

saw the police car there, her disappointment over not finding answers turned into concern.

As soon as she stepped onto the deck, Cassidy met her.

"What's going on?" Serena's gaze traveled beyond the police chief to the open door of her home. "You're in my camper."

"We have a warrant." It almost sounded like an apology in Cassidy's voice as she held up a piece of paper in her hands.

"Why would you have a warrant for my camper?" The answer was right there on the edge of Serena's reasoning. She just didn't want to accept it.

"Unfortunately, Serena, you're a person of interest in our investigation. There's enough evidence that we felt compelled to look further into your belongings for any indication you might be involved."

Serena felt her head spin and leaned against the railing. Though she had been halfway expecting it, hearing the words out loud made her feel lightheaded.

"And why is that?"

Cassidy stepped closer. "My initial assumption was correct. There were needle marks on the packaging on several different treats. It almost looked like some kind of poison was injected into them."

"Are you saying that's how Arnie died? Poison was injected in through the wrapper?" That sounded so horrible to hear it said aloud. How was this possible?

Cassidy shifted on the deck, using the pad of paper in her hands to fan her face as the summer sun bore down on them. "We're still investigating, of course. But there was enough evidence that we needed to check your place."

"You don't really think I did this, do you?" Serena stared at Cassidy, afraid that her friend might actually think she was guilty. Not that Cassidy would probably consider Serena a friend. But still.

"It doesn't matter what I think, Serena. I have to follow the evidence. It's my job." She stopped fanning her face long enough to frown.

"You know I didn't do this. If word gets out, my business will be destroyed. In fact, I'm losing so much money right now that I'm going to have a hard time paying my bills. Don't you care about that?"

"I know. And I'm sorry. I really am. But I would be doing an injustice to this whole community if I let my personal relationships dictate how I did my job.

Do you understand?" Cassidy's gaze latched onto hers.

Serena nodded and stepped back. She did understand. She wanted to be mad, but she couldn't. Cassidy spoke the truth.

Instead, Serena picked up Scoops and held the dog to her chest, finding comfort in her furry friend.

But her eyes widened when she saw another officer leave the camper with her computer.

"Why are you taking that?" Her voice screeched up another octave.

"Because we need to search it," Cassidy said.

"Why would you need to search my computer? It's a laptop—hardly big enough to hide a poison inside."

"To see if you were doing any kind of searches on poisons." Cassidy's voice sounded low and soft.

Serena crossed her arms. "I wasn't. I'll save you the time."

"You know we have to see that for ourselves."

Serena shook her head, feeling a headache coming on. Could this get any worse? "I can't believe this."

"I know. Let us do our jobs. If you didn't do anything, the evidence should show that. But I have to ask, who else might have had access to your ice cream truck?"

"No one. I keep it locked up."

"For now, I think we have everything we need," Cassidy said. "I'll be in touch."

Serena nodded, hating how heavy her entire body felt at the moment. "Okay."

Cassidy paused before she walked away. "And Serena? If you need anything, let me know. I mean it. If you find yourself running short on money or food or any necessities? I'll make sure you're taken care of, okay?"

Serena nodded, feeling a surge of gratitude. She knew Cassidy was a good person. She just hated to be on the wrong side of the law right now.

Especially since she was innocent.

———

SERENA STAYED in the camper long enough to feed and water Scoops, check her social media, and turn in her latest article about the shell art on the beach. Of course, she had to do all of that on her phone since the police had taken her computer.

She'd just begun to ponder her next steps when

she heard a knock on the door. When she answered, she was surprised to see Webster standing there.

"I just heard. How are you doing?"

She narrowed her eyes in confusion. "How in the world did you hear?"

"I was listening to the police scanner, of course."

Of *course*. "I didn't do this."

"I know you didn't."

Serena studied him a moment. His eyes looked sincere. Webster hadn't come here to gloat, she realized. He'd come here as a friend.

"Would you like to come in?" she asked.

He'd never been inside her place before. It wasn't exactly set up for entertaining.

"I was actually going to head down to the pier." He held up a picnic basket. "I have enough food for two. You want to join me?"

"Are you sure you want to be seen with someone who might be thought of as the potential ice cream killer?"

"I think I'll be fine." He offered a compassionate smile.

After staring at him for another moment, Serena finally nodded. "Getting out of the house sounds like a good idea. But I have to admit, there's a part of me that doesn't even want to show my face around here anymore."

"Then I think getting out might be your best option. Don't hide like you're guilty."

Webster was right. If she acted guilty, people might think she was guilty. She couldn't feed the hype.

Instead, Serena picked up her dog and stepped outside. "You driving?"

"Absolutely."

They climbed into Webster's sedan and started down the road.

Ten minutes later, they had parked and walked across the sand to the pier. A lot of people were already out. Some had brought their grills. Others had brought their fishing poles. Still others had stretched hammocks across the pilings of the pier and relaxed there now. As the sun began to set, no doubt people would be starting their bonfires.

Webster spread out a blanket for them and motioned for Serena to sit. "You just relax. You've got enough on your mind. I wanted to make this easy on you."

She didn't argue. She sat on one corner and Webster sat on the other with the picnic basket between them. He began pulling out some homemade chicken salad sandwiches, fresh fruit, and chips. He even pulled out a couple gourmet dog treats for Scoops from a shop in town.

"This chicken salad looks great." She grabbed a sandwich and held it up. It looked tasty with its grapes, nuts, and crusty bread. "Did you make these?"

"As a matter of fact, I did. When you're a single guy you have to learn to cook, especially if you want to try to stay in shape."

Funny, she had never thought of Webster as someone who cared about being in shape. But, now that he mentioned it, he wasn't flabby. His arms did have some definition to them.

Maybe he wasn't the total bookworm she'd assumed.

"How do you like Lantern Beach?" she asked, nibbling on her late lunch/early dinner as the seagulls began to circle overhead. Those greedy birds could spot food a mile away. Now they weren't going to let up, were they?

"I'm starting to get a better idea of what life is like here. I think I could get used to it."

A sense of disappointment mingled with a thrill of pleasure. It made no sense. If Serena was smart, she would want him to get out of town as soon as possible so she could become the new newspaper editor. But, in the short amount of time they had known each other, he'd already become somewhat of a friend.

Serena hated the fact that her feelings were torn on the subject. It was easier when things were black and white. Chocolate and vanilla. Mostly, they seemed swirled now.

"I have to admit that I thought things would be boring here," he continued, grabbing a plastic fork and stabbing a piece of watermelon. "But they've been anything but."

Serena offered a half eye roll. "Lantern Beach is never boring. As peaceful as these shores look and as friendly as the locals might be, the isolation of this place also seems to bring out the worst in some people."

She took another bite of her sandwich, and they enjoyed a few minutes of silence. What Serena wanted to ask was why Webster had really come to the island.

It seemed so weird that he'd gone from working at such large metropolitan newspapers, to coming to this small town where the newspaper would barely be able to support a mortgage. Right now, it wasn't a problem because he was living with his aunt. But the man was a mystery to her.

Serena knew if she asked him any questions about himself that he would also ask too many questions about her.

"I like the Dorothy outfit," Webster said. "I used to love that movie when I was a kid."

"Me too."

As if Webster could read her mind, he lowered his cup of fruit salad and said, "I have to admit that I'm really curious about why you wear different outfits every day."

And there it was. The personal questions. The ones she wanted to avoid.

"Can't a girl just like to mix up her wardrobe?" Serena kept it simple, hoping he wouldn't probe anymore, and then stuffed her face with another bite of sandwich.

"I'm a reporter. I like to get to the root of things. So, yes, you can definitely enjoy mixing up your wardrobe. But is that all there is to it?" He took a long sip of his water, but his gaze never left Serena.

He wasn't going to drop this. Maybe this picnic was a terrible idea. The last thing Serena wanted to do was reopen the gaping wounds caused by her past and expose herself to her competition.

Before she had the chance to respond, someone in the distance caught her eye. She grabbed Webster's arm and pointed down the beach. "Do you recognize that man?"

Webster followed her gaze and froze. "Isn't that one of the co-owners of Arnie's company? One of the founders whose photos we saw on the Rippled website?"

"That's who it looks like to me." The two of them exchanged a glance. "We need to talk to him. Now."

CHAPTER EIGHT

SCOOPS STAYED on her heels as Serena raced across the sand. Running on the beach was harder than people might think, especially if a person was trying to be graceful. Thankfully, Serena didn't care because her body shifted in all kinds of awkward ways on the uneven ground.

Webster surged ahead of her and called out, "Hey!"

The man in question looked back at them, and his eyes widened as he stood on the shore with various items placed around him.

Serena recognized him. He was the fitness buff at the company.

That meant, if he started to run, Serena probably couldn't catch him.

Instead, he raised one hand as if he were innocent and kept a fishing pole in the other.

Serena, Webster, and Scoops all stopped in front of him, panting and out of breath and put to shame by this man's muscles.

"Can I help you?" he asked, setting the pole into a holder that had been buried in the sand.

"You're Skip Williams," Webster said, drawing in another breath.

"Do I know you all?" He stared at them in obvious confusion.

The man looked just as nice in person as he did in his photo. Like a real-life Ken doll. A Ken doll who went fishing.

It seemed like a weird thing for a killer to be doing.

"You work with Arnie Blankenship," Serena said, straightening her Dorothy dress and tugging on one of the loose braids behind her ear.

The man's eyes widened even more. "That's right. I've been looking for him, but he hasn't answered his phone. How did you know that?"

Serena stared at him, trying to ascertain whether or not he was telling the truth right now. She couldn't be sure. If he was lying, he seemed really calm.

"You've been trying to call Arnie?" she asked instead, avoiding his question.

"That's right. I came to the island to talk to him, but I haven't been able to figure out where he's staying."

Serena and Webster exchanged another glance.

"I take it the two of you know him?" The man's hands went to his hips and the sun hit his very developed muscles.

"You really haven't talked to him in a few days?" Webster asked, squinting against the glare off the ocean.

"No, I haven't." The man crossed his bulky arms, his posture becoming more standoffish by the moment. "What's going on here? Who are you two?"

"One more question first," Serena said. "When did you get into town?"

"I flew down to Norfolk yesterday and rented a car to drive down here," he said. "A black Ford Explorer, to be exact. How is that relevant to anything?"

If his story checked out, then he wouldn't have been here when Arnie was murdered.

"We're sorry to let you know this, but Arnie is . . ." Webster frowned and softened his voice. "Arnie is dead."

Serena was thankful that Webster had shared the news so she didn't have to. But she watched Skip's face as he processed the news.

He blinked and then shook his head, as if he'd been sincerely clueless. "You can't be serious."

"Don't you read the newspaper?" Serena asked, surprised the news hadn't reached him yet.

"There's a newspaper around here?"

"It's digital," Webster said. "But that's beside the point right now. Arnie's body was found yesterday in his home here."

Skip ran a hand over his face as shock captured his features. "I can't believe this. What happened?"

"The police are trying to figure it out still," Serena said. "They think he could have been poisoned."

"Poisoned?" The word came out louder than Skip must have intended because he glanced around as people nearby started to stare. He stepped closer. "Poisoned by what?"

"They're still trying to figure that out," Serena said.

Skip shook his head before his shoulders slumped. "I can't believe this. Can't believe Arnie is gone."

"It seems strange that you would come all the

way to Lantern Beach to talk to him without mentioning something to him first," Serena said.

"Our company had a big shake-up about a month ago, and we let him go. But we realized what a mistake that was. I came here to beg for forgiveness and ask him to come back and work for us."

"Again, you just couldn't have called him?" Serena asked.

"He wasn't taking my calls. Then again, I just started trying to contact him a couple days ago." His face slashed with pain. "I guess I know why now."

SERENA, Webster, and Scoops got back to their picnic only to discover a burly Rottweiler had eaten the rest of their food. A man and woman stood there with apologetic looks on their faces as they tried to pull their dog away.

"We're so sorry," the man said. "The food must have smelled good, because we just couldn't pull him away."

Webster frowned as he stared at the now empty picnic basket. "It's okay."

After exchanging a few more words with the couple, the food thief and his people walked away.

Serena looked at Webster. "What now?"

"How about we forget about lunch, and we go get ice cream? Or is that too hard for you?"

"Ice cream should never be a source of stress," she said. "Let's go."

They gathered their things and climbed back into Webster's car. A few minutes later, Webster, Serena, and Scoops were seated outside one of the other ice cream establishments on the island.

They'd both gotten milkshakes, and Scoops had gotten some broken ice cream cone pieces an employee offered him. Scoops wasn't complaining as he crunched on the waffle cone.

"So what do you think about what this Skip guy told us?" Serena asked, watching Webster's face. She wanted to know his take on their conversation with Skip. Had he seen something she hadn't?

"The man seemed sincere. He could have been a good actor, though. Does he match the size of the man you saw hiding at the campground?"

Serena shrugged. "It's hard to say. It was dark outside and hard to see anything . . ."

"Understandable."

"I'm surprised he hadn't heard about Arnie's death," Serena said. "Wouldn't Cassidy have delivered a death notification to Arnie's family?"

"*If* Arnie had family. It didn't sound like he was married. Maybe his next of kin was a sibling or something. They may not have thought about telling his former coworkers what happened. Not yet, at least." Webster paused. "What do you think?"

Serena replayed their talk. "I agree. He looked genuinely surprised when we told him the news about Arnie. My only problem was that it seems like too much of a coincidence that he was here when it happened."

Webster took a long sip of his drink. "I agree. Skip shows up here right when a murder happens? Besides, he seems like he would be the best suspect in this investigation."

"My thoughts exactly. Since they have a personal connection, then it seems like he would have the best motive." Serena used her straw to stir the ice cream in her cup. "So where do we go from here?"

"We can try to figure out where Skip is staying and then watch him," Webster said.

Serena nodded. "I like how you think. But how are we going to find out where he's staying?"

"I saw the black SUV that Skip mentioned renting. It was in the lot near the pier. I say we drive around until we find it and then we see what happens. Besides, we don't have any more suspects at this point, do we?"

Serena shook her head and took another sip of her chocolate shake. "No, as a matter of fact we don't. Let's do it."

CHAPTER NINE

THERE WERE some perks to living on a small island. For starters, a person could canvas the entire town in about two hours.

That's exactly what Serena and Webster had done.

Finally, in one of the more moderately sized rentals on the ocean side, they located Skip's SUV in a driveway.

"That's got to be it," Serena muttered.

Webster found a parking space on the side of the sandy street and angled his car so they could see the SUV. Then they settled back to watch what this Skip guy would do.

"This could be a waste of time," Serena told

Webster, leaning back in the seat and giving him fair warning.

"I know. But it might not be."

"I like the way you think," Serena said.

Webster had been a real lifesaver lately, and she had to appreciate that. As much as she liked to give him a hard time, he had some finer qualities also.

"I used to deliver papers when I was a teenager," Webster said. "It's part of what made me want to be a journalist, to be honest."

Serena turned to him. "Is that right?"

"I suppose it wasn't much different from what you do as an ice cream lady. We both have eyes and ears on the community around us."

"Yes, we do." Finally, someone who got her.

"I remember one time, there was an older lady who always opened the door to get her newspaper when I came by at 6:00 a.m. every day. But one morning, she didn't."

"What happened?" Serena turned toward him, interested in hearing his story.

"I became concerned. So I parked my bike and walked up to her door. I thought maybe she was sick. But when I knocked, she didn't answer."

"Did you call the police? 911?"

"I did eventually. But I glanced inside first and

saw her lying on the floor. I knew something was wrong. When I tried the door, it was unlocked. Turns out, she'd had a heart attack. I was able to give her CPR until the medics arrived."

Serena rubbed Scoops's head. "Did she live?"

"As a matter of fact, she did. Do you know how I knew how to do CPR?"

"How?"

"I read an article about it. I was hooked after that moment, after realizing the power of words and information. I knew I wanted to do whatever I could to be on the front lines. To make a difference."

Serena's heart warmed just a little. Webster had actually given her a glimpse into his past.

"I like that story," she said. "Thank you for sharing."

He shrugged. "I'm not saying I'm a hero. But I am saying that small jobs that might seem inconsequential to some people are actually important in the grand scheme of things."

"I couldn't agree more." Her family thought selling ice cream was a silly little job. But Serena loved the life she'd made for herself here.

Just then, Serena's phone rang. She saw it was Cassidy, and her stomach tightened.

"Hello?" she answered.

"Serena," Cassidy said. "Where are you?"

"Uh . . ." She glanced at Skip's car. "Webster and I are just out and about in town. Why?"

"I need you to come down to the police station."

Her stomach tightened even more, a bad feeling brewing inside. "Is everything okay?"

"Just get down here. Now."

She ended the call and looked back at Webster. She had no idea what this was about, but she had no doubt that it wasn't good.

SERENA'S STOMACH twisted in knots as she walked into the police station. Webster and Scoops came with her, but they remained in the waiting area while Cassidy escorted her to an interrogation room.

As soon as Serena stepped inside the gray, gloomy room and the door was shut, she fought the urge to throw up.

She thought she liked to do things like solving mysteries and involving herself in crimes. But if this was what it felt like to do so, then she didn't like it. At all.

She imagined herself spending the rest of her days in jail for a murder she didn't commit. In jail, there would be no Instagram. There would be no dressing crazy different ways every day. There would be no watching YouTube videos or trying to figure out her future or how to redeem her past.

There would be no ice cream.

Cassidy lowered herself into the seat across the table from her.

"I'm dying here," Serena said, not wasting any time. "You've gotta tell me what's going on."

Cassidy leaned toward Serena. "Serena, would you like to tell me why you were doing computer searches on peanut allergies?"

Serena felt her eyes widen. "I wasn't."

"Serena . . ."

"I really wasn't." Serena's voice climbed with anxiety. "Why would I do that? What are you saying, Cassidy?"

"I'm saying that our computer tech found evidence that you did a search a few days ago on peanut allergies. Did Arnie Blankenship tell you that he was allergic to peanuts?"

The air left her lungs. "He was allergic to peanuts? I suppose that makes sense. He never ordered nutty buddies or anything that might have peanuts in them."

Cassidy didn't say anything, she just listened.

Facts began to click in Serena's mind. She needed to be careful what she said, but her mouth seemed to take on a mind of its own.

"So you're saying that Arnie had a peanut allergy and that the poison injected into my ice cream wasn't actually a poison but something peanut?"

Cassidy still didn't say anything.

"I have no reason for wanting Arnie dead. And I didn't do that internet search. And I didn't inject anything into my ice cream." Serena paused as her future flashed before her eyes. "Do I need to get a lawyer?"

The idea just seemed absurd.

"A lawyer might not be a bad idea, Serena."

Cassidy's words drove home reality, and Serena's head began to spin. "Cassidy, you can't possibly think—"

"I'm just telling you what the evidence says." Her voice sounded calm but cautious. Cassidy was trying to remain professional while still advising Serena, wasn't she? "And the evidence clearly shows that internet search on your computer."

"Well, I didn't do it. Someone is setting me up." Serena fought tears. How could this be happening? It was like a nightmare—a nightmare where someone made her look guilty.

"Why would someone want to make you look guilty?"

"So I could take the fall, I guess. The ice cream in my truck . . . it had been injected with something also?"

"We're still waiting to hear."

"Are you arresting me?" Dread pooled in Serena's stomach as she waited for Cassidy's response.

"Not yet."

"But you might?" Her voice climbed even higher.

Who would take care of Scoops?

"We're testing some cooking oil that was found in your house. When we get the results of that back, we'll know something more definite."

"Everyone has oil in their house." Cassidy's words made no sense.

"This was canola oil. At least, that's what the container said. The lab suspects it's actually peanut oil." Cassidy leveled her gaze with Serena, her eyes studying Serena's expression.

Serena's head began to spin. This couldn't be happening.

But it was.

She might actually take the fall for this.

CHAPTER TEN

SERENA DIDN'T SAY anything to Webster as she
left the interrogation room. Instead, she motioned
for him and Scoops to follow. She waited until they
were in his car with the doors closed and the AC
cranked before she spoke.

"The police think that I may have done this," she
told him. The words sounded surreal, even to her
own ears.

Webster's eyes widened. "What? Why?"

"It turns out Arnie had a peanut allergy, and they
think peanut oil was injected into the ice cream."
She buried her face in Scoops's fur, finding comfort
in the salty, sandy scent of the dog.

Everything felt dead around her. But it wasn't.

Everything was very much alive and just waiting for her demise.

Webster stared at her. "That's ridiculous. They should be able to prove that's not true pretty easily."

"That might be the case," Serena said. "But when the police checked my computer, they discovered some type of internet search on peanut allergies. And they think I replaced the oil in my cupboard with peanut oil."

His eyes became even wider. "Why would you do that?"

"I didn't."

"The only other option is that somebody set you up," Webster said.

"Exactly. But who would do that? Who would have that much of a vendetta against me and Arnie?"

"It might not have anything to do with you. Maybe the real killer just needed a fall guy."

Just then, another thought hit Serena. "When I was on my ice cream route two days ago, the last day that Arnie was alive, one of the moms who bought ice cream from me went through a big spiel about how her daughter had a nut allergy. We went through all the wrappers trying to figure out what this girl could or couldn't eat."

"Okay . . ."

"But if my ice cream had been tainted, the killer couldn't have known which treats Arnie was going to buy. That means that anybody who bought ice cream from me, thinking it was nut-free, could have actually gotten ice cream that was injected with peanut oil."

Webster's eyes widened. "That's not good. I can call Clemson and see if anybody came into the clinic with some type of anaphylactic reaction."

"You can do that," Serena said, her mind racing. "But I'm not sure he's going to give you any answers. I remember where this girl lived. Do you mind if we go pay her a visit?"

"Not at all. Just tell me where I need to go."

Serena rattled off the directions, and, five minutes later they pulled up to the house.

Serena didn't waste any time climbing from the car and hurrying toward the front door. She pounded on it and waited. Finally, Webster joined her, holding Scoops in his arms.

As soon as the mother opened the door, her face lit up with a smile. She reached forward and gave Scoops a pat on the head.

"What brings you two here?" the woman asked. "What a surprise."

Serena already felt a little better when she realized that the woman was acting fairly normal. If something had happened to her daughter, certainly she would be more frantic right now.

"I have to ask, is your daughter okay?" Serena started.

The woman froze, her hand on the door frame. "She's fine. Why?"

What was Serena supposed to say? She hadn't thought that far ahead. "I found out that one of the wrappers on my ice cream may have been misla-beled. The treat may have been processed in a peanut factory. As soon as I heard that, I became worried about your daughter. I couldn't remember exactly which ice cream products you finally picked out."

"She got an ice cream sandwich. But she's doing fine. No problems at all."

Serena let out a breath, relief washing through her. "I'm so glad to hear that. As soon as I found out, you were the first person I thought about."

"I really appreciate your concern. That means a lot. I mean, a peanut allergy can be a very scary thing, especially when you're a parent and you have to watch everything your child eats. But I assure you, she is feeling fine. Her reaction would have been instantaneous."

Serena smiled. "I'm so glad."

Before she could walk away, something behind the woman caught her eye. It was a box of . . . cell phones.

The woman followed her gaze. "Is everything okay?"

Serena shifted. "That's not something you see every day."

"I collect cell phones for a local women's shelter back home. I left a box here at the local library and picked them up earlier." The woman's eyes narrowed. "Is that a problem?"

Serena shook her head. "No . . . thank you again for your help."

She was going to keep those cell phones in mind . . . just in case they came into play later.

And, with that, Serena, Webster, and Scoops went back to his car.

At least, she could rest easier knowing her customers were okay.

"THAT'S good news that her daughter is fine," Webster said as they took off down the road again.

"It is." Serena was so grateful that no one else

had been harmed. Yet she wasn't ready to rest easy yet either. "But it doesn't make any sense. If someone poisoned all of my ice cream—and I say poisoned, when I suppose I really mean injected peanut oil—"

"—in this case, it's the same thing."

"Yes, it is," Serena continued. "If they did that to all of my ice cream because they were unsure about what Arnie would order, then other people could be feeling the effects of this."

"I agree."

Serena stared out the window at the various homes as they passed them. "So that makes me think that the ice cream was poisoned after Arnie had already purchased it."

Webster stole a quick glance at her. "But why would there be needle marks in the wrappers of your other ice cream then?"

"That's what I'm not sure about." Serena frowned, feeling a headache coming on. "All the pieces aren't fitting, are they?"

"This is all definitely a mystery."

She glanced at Webster, trying to read his expression as she asked her next question. "And do you really think that lady was collecting cell phones? I mean, someone heard Arnie arguing with someone about that very subject. Is it a coincidence?"

"I have no idea."

Serena's thoughts continued to race. What were they missing?

She wasn't sure. But there was one thing she could think of that they could do.

"Can we go back to Skip's place?" she asked. "I still want to keep an eye on him. I find his appearance here to be very suspicious."

Scoops barked, as if in agreement.

"It looks like it's two against one. Let's go."

They took their same position outside the man's house again.

They'd only been sitting there for ten minutes when they saw Skip emerge.

And he had two suitcases in tow.

"He's leaving," Serena muttered, her mind racing.

"You think he's getting out of town before he's caught?"

"It sounds like a good theory to me. I can't let him leave."

"What are you suggesting?"

Serena grabbed the door handle, determination surging in her. "I'm suggesting we go confront him. Right now."

Before Webster could stop her, Serena climbed

from the car and charged toward her number one suspect.

CHAPTER ELEVEN

"WHAT DO you think you're doing?" Serena called.

Skip stopped in his tracks, his luggage hovering over the back of his SUV as he froze. "I'm heading home to Pennsylvania. There's no reason for me to stay here anymore."

"Or are you leaving before people think that you're guilty?" she followed up as Webster and Scoops joined her.

Skip's eyes narrowed, and he stared at her. "Guilty of what?"

"Of killing Arnie Blankenship."

He straightened and shook his head. "Why would I kill Arnie? I wanted him to come back to the company."

"What if he refused?" Serena asked. "And what if

you wanted the ultimate act of revenge? After all, wasn't he the one who was funding your operations anyway? Without him on your payroll your whole company was in even bigger trouble."

"That's not true. Yes, he did fund most of our operations. But he also had the biggest salary because of that. We knew we couldn't keep going on like that. We needed to be self-sustaining. We were hoping to bring him back in a different capacity."

"Did you know he had a peanut allergy?" Serena continued.

"I did. He wasn't shy about telling people about it. Why?"

The man looked honestly surprised. But Serena still had to be careful here.

"Somebody injected peanut oil into his food. That's how he died."

Skip sagged against the SUV. "I had no idea. That's horrible."

"Did you talk to the police yet?" Webster asked. "Because maybe you have some insight that would help them."

"As a matter of fact, I did swing by the police station right after I talked to you guys. I have nothing to hide."

"It still just seems suspicious that you're leaving

right now." Serena crossed her arms as she waited for his response.

He let out a long breath. "Look, after you guys told me that he died, I actually went onto our company's email system. I found an email Arnie sent me a couple days ago."

"And?" Serena leaned forward, anxious to hear what he had to say.

"Arnie sent me a note about how he'd found a great new investment opportunity for some new tech. He was going to be pursuing that instead of coming back to our company."

"Interesting," Webster muttered.

"He's always been an indulgent kind of guy. If he sees something he wants, he goes after it. Nothing else matters."

"Like ice cream?" Serena frowned.

"Exactly like ice cream," Skip said. "He loved that stuff and was always bringing it in to work for people. He liked vacation homes also. That's why he bought a place here. But he also has a place in the mountains and another place on a lake. And he owns five vehicles. That's just the kind of guy Arnie is."

"So you think this new investment opportunity may have gotten him killed?" Webster asked.

Skip shrugged. "I couldn't tell you that. I'm not a cop, nor do I pretend to be one. I'll let them figure it out. But it does seem suspicious to me."

"Do you have any idea if this investment opportunity had anything to do with cell phones or if he'd need a patent for it?" Serena asked.

Skip shrugged. "I have no idea."

"Was there anything else suspicious in his emails?" Serena asked, knowing it was a long shot that he would share anything else.

"No, there wasn't. And if you want any more information, you're going to have to go to the police. I've already told you too much."

With that, he slammed the hatch closed and climbed into his driver's seat. With a slight wave, he took off down the road.

That was the end of that conversation.

Serena had learned a little bit more. But was it enough?

FIFTEEN MINUTES LATER, Serena, Webster, and Scoops sat outside on her deck drinking lemonade as the sun set.

"So where does this leave us?" Webster asked. "Are there any suspects left?"

"The only thing I can think of is that it's somebody we haven't identified yet. Really, there's so much that we don't even know about this Arnie guy. Meeting him, I would have never guessed him to be a shark. He seemed more like a dolphin."

"Maybe his death had something to do with this new investment opportunity he had come across."

"If that's true, then he could have met this potential adversary online. The man could have snuck into his house, poisoned him, and be long gone from this island right now. There's even a chance that nobody saw him come or go."

"But if that was true, then when would this person have had time to set you up?"

"If someone in the tech field really is involved in this, what if they hacked into my computer and set up that fake search?"

Webster shrugged. "I suppose if they're good enough, that's a possibility."

"The Brunette's husband is an entrepreneur. Plus, I still think Skip has the best motives here."

Serena took another long sip of lemonade, her thoughts still brewing. "You know what? Do you mind waiting out here for a second? I'm going to get this Dorothy outfit off and put something more comfortable on."

"No problem."

As Serena went inside to change, her gaze drifted to some bills she had left on her desk.

Too many more days without having any ice cream to sell, and she wouldn't have money to make ends meet. That was the reality of living life paycheck to paycheck.

Even though Skye officially owned this camper, there was still rent to pay on this spot, there were still electric bills to pay, college loans, and even a small amount of credit card debt.

What was she going to do if this didn't blow over?

The thoughts were still heavy on her mind as she went outside five minutes later dressed in sweatpants and a plain black T-shirt.

"I like the casual look," Webster said, one of his hands resting on Scoops's back.

She shrugged. "It's a little boring, but it's okay."

A moment of silence fell between them, and Serena's thoughts continued to move forward.

"You want to know why I always wear these different outfits?" Serena finally said.

"I'd be lying if I said I wasn't curious."

"The truth is, to look at me, people might think I'm normal. But deep down inside me, there's a rebel. I'm not like everybody else, and I know that. I know I'm different, that I march to the beat of my own drum."

Webster didn't say anything; he just listened.

"The area where I lived in Michigan was pretty affluent. I never really found a place to fit in while in school. The other kids realized that. By the fifth grade, the rest of my classmates saw me as a target. They made fun of me until I became a total outsider."

"In other words, they bullied you."

She nodded. "I suppose. For a while, I decided I was going to try to blend in. I was going to repress who I really was in order to try to fit. Eventually, the cracks began to peek through, though. I was right back to where I started—maybe even in a worse place. Once people realized I'd been being fake, then I *really* didn't fit in. At all. As soon as I graduated and I was able to get away from that place, I did."

"I can't say I blame you."

"When I came here to Lantern Beach, I realized that I had the opportunity to be anybody I wanted to be. I've always loved dressing up, and Halloween, and wearing costumes. One day, I decided to dress like a sailor, and I watched people's reactions. It was so much fun that I decided to do it again the next day, only dressing as someone different. Before I knew it, I had created this whole new persona of ever-changing characters. And it was fun. Kept people on their toes."

"And it kept people from seeing who you really were," Webster finished.

"I suppose it did that also. But there's a certain measure of safety in that. If people don't really know who I am, then they can't criticize me. Not the real me at least." Her words hung in the air, entirely too vulnerable for her comfort.

She'd never admitted any of that out loud before.

Webster turned toward her. "So are you happy with your current state of being?"

"I love the costumes. I love the makeup. And sometimes I even love feeling safe. But the truth is, I'm still figuring things out. I'm not really sure when that will pass."

"I'm sure most of us have a little bit of that uncertainty in our lives. I imagine as we get older and more settled that it becomes easier, though."

"I suppose it does." She glanced at him and smiled. "Anyway, thanks for listening. I haven't told anybody that since I moved here. It kind of feels good to get it off my chest."

"Why did you decide to bring it up now?"

"Because what if I do end up going to jail for all of this? Or if my business never bounces back? It's sobering, to say the least. I figured there needed to be at least one person here on this island who knows who I really am."

"Your Aunt Skye doesn't even know this?"

"Only bits and pieces, I suppose."

"Well, I'm honored that you shared this with me. Thank you."

Serena stood, exhausted from all of today's events and even exhausted from opening up her past. It had taken more energy than she thought it would. "I think I'm going to hit the hay now. It's been a long day."

Webster stood also and handed her his glass. "Thank you for the lemonade. We can catch up tomorrow for breakfast?"

She nodded. "That sounds good."

But deep inside, Serena wondered if she was even going to be available for breakfast.

What if she ended up in jail instead? Because all the evidence in the death of Arnie Blankenship pointed to her.

CHAPTER TWELVE

SERENA'S THOUGHTS had raced all night as she tried to put the pieces together.

She knew that whoever was behind Arnie's death had to have been in town for a while. Otherwise, it was like Webster said, the killer wouldn't have been able to set Serena up.

She also knew that Arnie had been fired. He was the financial and tech guy for the company. He had come across another opportunity he was excited about. Serena had no idea what that might be, but maybe he was working on it while he was here.

In fact, maybe the person who was behind his death was also a tech genius. After all, whoever had set her up had planted that peanut allergy search on her computer.

Whoever it was, he knew that Serena was the ice cream lady and that Arnie bought treats from her nearly every day and that he had a serious peanut allergy. That was the only reason the killer was able to use those very treats to poison Arnie.

Brunette's husband had heard him arguing with someone the day before he died, something about a cell phone. Brunette's husband was also an entrepreneur, so maybe he had come forward with some kind of idea and there had been an argument. Plus, Brunette's husband would know that Arnie liked to buy a lot of ice cream treats from Serena every day.

A theory came together in her mind. What if someone had come to Arnie and presented him with a new idea, and Arnie had essentially stolen it from this person? What if he had gone as far as to file a patent for the idea? Maybe it was a new app. That's why the word cell phone had been mentioned. Apps were generally used on cell phones, after all.

When Serena put all of that together, there was only one person who made sense.

Bright and early the next morning, Serena and Scoops rode her bike down to Arnie Blankenship's house. She parked her bike near the bushes where nobody would see it and walked around the outside of the space.

At the back of the property, a thick patch of underbrush and trees stretched. A small path, just narrow enough for Serena to get through, cut between some of the trees. As she examined the space, she saw footprints there.

She slipped through and stood on the edge of the foliage.

A small cottage sat on the other side. She had a feeling that the person who had killed Arnie lived there.

Serena knew better than to try to take this on herself.

But did she have enough evidence to call Cassidy? Basically, she was going off intuition and a vague theory right now.

She glanced at her watch. She had thirty minutes until she was supposed to meet Webster. Maybe she should talk this through with him before she did anything rash.

She pulled out her phone and punched in his number. Before he could say hello, she poured her theory out to him.

"Serena, I want to talk to you about that, but there's really something that I need to tell you—"

What else could he possibly need to chat about at a time like this? "We'll have to talk about whatever that is later. Right now, I need to know what to do. I'm standing outside the potential killer's house."

"First, you need to leave. Then you need to call Cassidy. If you're right, then you don't want to put yourself in danger."

"But all the evidence I have is simply circumstantial."

"But what you said makes sense," Webster said. "I think it has some validity. You really need to call Cassidy."

She nodded, knowing what he said was true. "Okay. I'll do that. And thank you, Webster, for being such a good friend and for listening to me. I know I was really uncertain about you coming to this island at first but—"

"Serena, you really need to listen to what I have to say."

She continued staring at the house where Arnie's supposed killer lived, but she saw no movement there. Maybe she had a couple more minutes to get this conversation out of the way. "What's going on, Webster?"

"I didn't have anything to do with the article that ran in today's online paper."

Serena froze. What was he talking about?

"You haven't seen it yet then, huh?" Webster asked.

"No, I had other things on my mind."

"Ernestine wrote an article about Arnie's death."

A bad feeling welled in Serena's stomach. "What are you saying, Webster?"

"I talked things over last night with Ernestine, trying to get her feel for all of this. I had no idea she was going to use what I told her in the article."

Worst-case scenarios flashed in her mind. "Webster, you're going to need to spell this out for me some more."

"Ernestine ran an article about Arnie's murder. She said that the police had a suspect but no arrest had been made. She even mentioned something about a computer search for a peanut allergy."

Serena sucked in a breath as betrayal sliced through her. "She was talking about me?"

"She didn't use your name."

"How could you do this to me?" Serena felt like she was back in high school again. Was there anybody she could truly trust? Anybody who was looking out for her? Or did everybody only care about themselves?

"It wasn't like that, Serena. Ernestine said she

thought the public had the right to know what was going on."

Serena felt a headache coming on and pulled the phone away from her ear. She could be mature about this. She drew in a deep breath, trying to gather herself before talking to Webster again.

There was no use. She was too angry to say anything nice. "I'm sorry, but I've gotta go."

"Wait, Serena. Where are you?"

Before she could answer him, a footstep sounded behind her.

The next instant, something smashed into her head and everything went black.

———

WHEN SERENA OPENED HER EYES, she had no idea where she was.

She glanced around, but nothing looked familiar.

Then everything flooded back to her.

Locating the house. Finding the killer. Learning that Webster had betrayed her after she had finally opened up. Then feeling something hit her.

She tried to push herself up, but everything spun around her. Her head was killing her right now.

Where was Scoops? The question struck her like a lightning bolt.

She glanced around. She was in an outdated bedroom with one window that had been covered with heavy drapes. There was a double bed with a burgundy bedspread and an old dresser that looked left over from the seventies.

But her dog was nowhere to be seen.

Serena had been holding the canine when she'd been talking on the phone to Webster. But then someone had hit her over the head and . . .

Had the killer grabbed Scoops also?

Concern pounded through her. She prayed that her dog was okay. She prayed *she* would be okay.

What was going on here?

Just then, the door opened, and someone stepped inside.

She sucked in a breath. It was just who Serena thought it would be.

Blue Raspberry.

She rubbed her head and backed toward the wall as he took another step toward her. His hands were empty, but that didn't mean he didn't have something up his sleeve—literally or figuratively.

"What do you think you're doing?" Her voice cracked as the question left her lips.

"I could ask you the same thing." His gaze looked off, didn't seem at one with reality as he stared down at her. "You were never supposed to get involved with this."

"I was only trying to find answers," she said. Who would have thought the process would be so dangerous?

"People need to mind their own business."

"You killed Arnie," she muttered, all doubt leaving her mind.

"I had no choice." His nostrils flared. "He stole something that should have been mine."

"You developed some new tech that Arnie was going to claim as his own, right?" Blue Raspberry had mentioned how Arnie was a computer genius.

"That's right. The two of us met on the beach one night, and I told him about an app I'd developed a prototype for. I just needed some additional funding in order to begin the process of software architecture planning and iOS development. Arnie said he might be able to help me."

"Then what happened?"

"He told me to come over to his house so we could talk about it more. When I told him the full scope of my idea, he was excited. He said he wanted to play with some ideas on how to properly develop it. Asked me about market research. He said all the right things."

"But his intentions weren't what they appeared, were they?" Serena asked.

Blue Raspberry's face reddened. "I didn't hear anything from him for a couple days. So I went back to his place to see how it was going, and Arnie tried to convince me that he could take the idea and run with it."

"That's what you wanted, right?"

"Initially, yes. But then I saw that he was applying for a patent on my idea. He was going to steal from me, to take all the credit. So I confronted him."

She could feel his temper rising and knew that wasn't a good thing. "What was this idea exactly?"

That was the one thing she hadn't been able to figure out. Did that idea somehow tie in with how the killer had gotten away with all of this?

Blue Raspberry's eyes lit with excitement. "I came up with a new app that lets people record and listen in on phone calls. All you have to do is have the phone number of the person you want to eaves-drop on. This app lets you hijack their conversation and hear everything. It's amazing, if I do say so myself."

"Why would you want to do that? I don't understand."

His gaze darkened again. "I could have saved myself a lot of heartache if I'd had that before my girlfriend dumped me. I would have known she was talking to someone else."

Serena blanched at his simple explanation. There wasn't even a touch of guilt in his voice. "That sounds intrusive. And illegal."

"It's mostly for people who suspect their spouse or boyfriend is cheating on them. It's a way to learn the truth about what's happening."

"You can patent that?"

"I wanted to patent part of the technology. I'd be able to sell it later to the government or other people who needed to use it." His gaze locked with hers. "It was the way that I learned that you thought I was guilty."

"You overheard my conversation with Webster this morning when I told him I had it figured out, didn't you?" Shock raced through her as a better mental image formed.

Blue Raspberry nodded, a grin spreading across his face. "Every word of it. My prototype works. I even heard you saying you were going to The Crazy Chefette that one day when I 'accidentally' ran into you there. I could overhear the conversations with police as well, and I made sure I stayed one step ahead."

"You've been trying to set me up this whole time."

Another emotion flashed in his eyes. Satisfaction? Approval?

Serena couldn't be sure.

"Someone had to take the fall for it, and I didn't want it to be me," the man said. "I didn't think that you were going to push back so much, though. I just figured somebody would think Arnie accidentally ate some peanuts and then died. But it turned into much more than that."

"Let's go back to the beginning for a minute. You discovered that Arnie had stolen your tech, and you felt powerless to do anything about it. Is that right?"

"That's right. He just mocked me when I said he wasn't going to be able to take my idea and run with it. I told him I was going to sue him. He laughed and said he had more money than I ever would."

"So you killed him? How did things turn deadly so quickly? And how did you know he had a peanut allergy?"

"He was blabbering on and on about it when we

ran into each other at the beach, and I was eating a peanut butter sandwich."

"How serendipitous."

"I needed another plan before he made millions off my idea. That's when I snuck into his house and injected the treats that he had in his freezer with peanut oil. He ate one of them and went into anaphylactic shock. But I'd taken all his EpiPens and hid them so he couldn't help himself. Then, I watched in the shadows as he died."

Serena shuddered as she imagined it playing out. This man was more heartless than she'd imagined. "Then what?"

"Then I posed Arnie at the table with all of the ice cream treats around him so it would be clear what had happened. It was supposed to be easy. End of story." His gaze darkened. "Until you came along."

"So you were going to walk away with this tech and leave me looking like the bad guy?"

"That's right. While you were in Arnie's house, discovering his dead body, I sneaked into your ice cream truck. I tampered with the rest of your treats, just in case the police investigated you. One of the smartest things I ever did."

Serena felt the anger burning inside her, but she knew she had to keep it under control. The best thing she could do right now was to buy more time. "You left the patent information."

"It was in his name. I couldn't do anything with it."

"What about the red sedan? I don't understand why it was outside the house?"

"I needed something to throw people off. I like to walk the island at night. I just happened to try to open that car door. It was unlocked. I found the key under the mat. A few days later, I decided it was the perfect way to throw the police off."

Serena swallowed, still trying to buy some time. "I'm surprised you just didn't leave the island."

"There's some coding for this new app that I haven't been able to find. I need to get into Arnie's house and onto his computer. His firewall was too strong for me to crack. I figured if the police were distracted by investigating you, that it might give me the opportunity I needed."

"And I guess you haven't had that chance yet? Even though you set up that fake internet search on my computer and substituted peanut oil for my oil?"

"That's right. Plus, I'm waiting to see if the police will return his computer. It's been down at the station."

"Too bad, too sad."

His gaze narrowed. "Don't worry, I'm going to think of Plan B. But first, I need to figure out how to get rid of you."

"You're going to kill me?" Serena scooted back farther until her back hit the wall. Fear rushed through her as she realized she was running out of time.

"I don't want to kill you." He stepped toward her, his face still twisted with disgust. "But I don't know how else to get rid of you."

"Well, I'm not allergic to peanuts, if that's what you're thinking." She tried to scoot back farther but there was nowhere to go. At least she hadn't been tied up. Then again, maybe that would have left evidence or possible bruising.

She glanced around, looking for a weapon. There was nothing. Not even a lamp to grab.

"I can set it up that you looked desperate," Blue Raspberry said. "Maybe you couldn't stand the thought of being discovered and decided you couldn't take it anymore. I'm thinking I can leave your body in the ice cream truck."

Her throat tightened even more. "You can't possibly think that's going to work. People who know me know that I'd never take my own life."

"I don't know what to think yet. But I'm going to

think of something." Blue Raspberry stretched out his hand, and a pill rested in his palm. "For starters, take this."

Serena stared at the blue tablet. "What is it?"

"Initially, it will just put you to sleep."

She sucked in a quick breath as a better mental image began to form. "I'm not taking that."

"Come on. Don't make this harder. Just take the pill."

"I won't." Serena wasn't going to make this easy on him. She would go out kicking and screaming.

He stepped closer to her, kneeling down beside her, and then raised the pill to her mouth. "Don't make me force you to do this."

"I'm not taking the pill."

Something changed on his face, and anger flashed across his features. He lifted the pill to her lips and tried to shove it into her mouth.

As he did, Serena kicked, hitting his arm. The pill went flying across the room.

The action threw Blue Raspberry off guard, for a moment at least.

The next instant, he grabbed the pill from the carpet and held it to her face. "I said, take this!"

Just as he tried to shove it into her mouth again, the door behind them flew open.

"Police! Stop where you are and put your hands up!" Cassidy Chambers stood there.

Blue Raspberry froze.

Serena watched, uncertain what he would do.

To her surprise, he raised his hands in the air and slowly turned.

Cassidy cuffed him as she began to read him his rights.

As she did, she glanced at Serena. "You okay?"

Serena nodded and rubbed her throat. "I'm fine."

"I'll be back to talk to you in a minute."

As Blue Raspberry was escorted from the room, Webster stepped inside, Scoops nestled in his arms. Worry stretched through the lines on his forehead as he stared at her.

"Scoops came and found me at The Crazy Chefette," he started. "The dog practically led me the entire way here until I found you."

Serena took the dog from him and hugged the canine to her chest. "You're the best, Scoops."

But as she glanced at Webster, she realized she could not say the same for him.

He'd betrayed her.

Just like most of the people in her life.

CHAPTER THIRTEEN

TWO HOURS LATER, Cassidy had taken Serena's statement, and Blue Raspberry had been arrested and taken to the police station.

It looked like this was a closed case after all.

As Serena stood outside Blue Raspberry's house, she rubbed Scoops's head, thankful for the dog. He'd saved her life by running to find help. The dog was like a guardian angel.

Serena heard a footstep behind her, and she knew without turning that it was Webster. He'd been trying to talk to her since all this happened.

Serena wasn't sure she wanted to talk to him, though.

Once she'd had a free moment, she read the

article he'd mentioned. Everything Webster told her was correct.

Ernestine had indeed printed that story about Arnie Blankenship and had mentioned that the police had a suspect in their sights. Even though Serena hadn't been directly mentioned, people would be able to piece together the facts.

"Serena, can you talk to me, please?" Webster asked, pausing in the shade behind her.

She might as well just get this over with. She slowly turned until she could see him, see the remorse on his face. Remorse wasn't going to be enough right now.

She hugged Scoops closer and narrowed her eyes as she looked at him. "I don't know what else you can say."

Webster started to reach for her but dropped his hand back down to his side. "You have to believe me when I say that I had no idea my aunt was going to write an article on this."

"How could Ernestine do this?" Serena hadn't exactly thought of the woman as a friend, but she'd never expected her capable of this. Weren't people supposed to look out for their own? To protect those in their circle?

"You have to look at it from her perspective,"

Webster said. "It would be an injustice to the people on this island if she didn't report this news just because she likes you—just like it would have been an injustice if Cassidy hadn't questioned you because you're one of her friends."

"But doesn't loyalty mean anything?"

"Do you want the bad guys to get away with something just because of who they know?"

Serena narrowed her eyes even more. "No, but I'm not a bad guy."

"And that's all going to come out. Especially now that this guy has been arrested. But don't people deserve to know the truth?"

Serena didn't even know what to say. The logical part of her said yes, of course, people deserved to know the truth. But another part of her didn't want to be on that side of justice. This was her livelihood that was at stake. Her life. Her reputation. All of that could be ruined because of this article.

What would Serena have done if the roles had been reversed? She'd like to say that her loyalty to people she cared about would win. But that would make her a terrible journalist if that was true.

Weren't journalists, by their very nature, supposed to be objective? And if a journalist wasn't objective, then they also weren't trustworthy, right? Emotion and logic collided inside her.

"I guess I know what you're saying." Serena frowned. "But that still doesn't exactly make me want to be a part of this newspaper anymore."

Webster stepped closer. "I need you on my team, Serena."

She lifted her chin as she observed him. His gaze looked sincere, and his drooped shoulders showed regret. But she wasn't letting him off the hook that easily. "And why do you need me on your team?"

"You're a good reporter. You have good instincts. You're driven. You add a lot to this island and to the newspaper."

That might be true but . . . "Do you think anyone's going to trust me now? Or will they always think of me as a potential ice cream killer?"

"Are you kidding? You're going to be the hero. When people learn that you cracked this case, you're going to sell more ice cream than ever."

"I'm not sure about that." But Serena liked the sound of it. A spike of hope spread through her.

"Don't give up on me." Webster stepped closer, his eyes imploring hers. "Please."

Something about the way he said the words made Serena wonder if there was more to his story.

She still didn't know why he had come to this island. But she knew there was a story there, and she hoped Webster would share that sometime.

"Good job out there, Serena." Cassidy stepped from the house where she and her officers had been collecting evidence. "You helped crack this case."

She looked up at the woman who'd become somewhat of a role model to her. In many ways, Serena had tried to follow in her footsteps— starting with taking over Elsa when Cassidy had become police chief. But Serena had a long way to go before she was ready to truly start solving crimes.

"Does that mean I'm all clear now?" Serena asked.

"You're all clear. John Belk just confessed to everything that happened."

John Belk? That had been Blue Raspberry's name? Serena liked her nickname for the man better. John Belk seemed too ordinary.

"Do you think I can get a quote from you for our follow-up article?" Webster asked, pulling a recorder from his pocket.

Cassidy nodded. "Of course. And it's going to be about how Serena Lavinia helped to solve this. She and her dog."

Serena's heart lifted. Maybe things would work out after all.

As Scoops wiggled in her arms, she placed the dog on the driveway and watched as he sniffed everyone's feet.

Sometimes, people needed a shake-up in their lives before they could move forward.

Now that this case was behind her, Serena planned on focusing on the future. On being the best journalist she could be. About what new character she could pose as on her ice cream routes. About how she could make this community a better place.

She might even try to figure out how she and Webster could best work together as a team.

She glanced over at him as he played with Scoops.

Maybe.

COMING NEXT: BOMB POP THREAT

ALSO BY CHRISTY BARRITT:

YOU ALSO MIGHT ENJOY...

LANTERN BEACH MYSTERIES

Hidden Currents

You can take the detective out of the investigation, but you can't take the investigator out of the detective. A notorious gang puts a bounty on Detective Cady Matthews's head after she takes down their leader, leaving her no choice but to hide until she can testify at trial. But her temporary home across the country on a remote North Carolina island isn't as peaceful as she initially thinks. Living under the new identity of Cassidy Livingston, she struggles to keep her investigative skills tucked away, especially after a body washes ashore. When local police bungle the murder investigation, she can't resist stepping in. But

Cassidy is supposed to be keeping a low profile. One wrong move could lead to both her discovery and her demise. Can she bring justice to the island . . . or will the hidden currents surrounding her pull her under for good?

Flood Watch

The tide is high, and so is the danger on Lantern Beach. Still in hiding after infiltrating a dangerous gang, Cassidy Livingston just has to make it a few more months before she can testify at trial and resume her old life. But trouble keeps finding her, and Cassidy is pulled into a local investigation after a man mysteriously disappears from the island she now calls home. A recurring nightmare from her time undercover only muddies things, as does a visit from the parents of her handsome ex-Navy SEAL neighbor. When a friend's life is threatened, Cassidy must make choices that put her on the verge of blowing her cover. With a flood watch on her emotions and her life in a tangle, will Cassidy find the truth? Or will her past finally drown her?

Storm Surge

A storm is brewing hundreds of miles away, but its effects are devastating even from afar. Laid-back, loose, and light: that's Cassidy Livingston's new motto. But when a makeshift boat with a bloody cloth inside washes ashore near her oceanfront home, her detective instincts shift into gear . . . again. Seeking clues isn't the only thing on her mind—romance is heating up with next-door neighbor and former Navy SEAL Ty Chambers as well. Her heart wants the love and stability she's longed for her entire life. But her hidden identity only leads to a tidal wave of turbulence. As more answers emerge about the boat, the danger around her rises, creating a treacherous swell that threatens to reveal her past. Can Cassidy mind her own business, or will the storm surge of violence and corruption that has washed ashore on Lantern Beach leave her life in wreckage?

Dangerous Waters

Danger lurks on the horizon, leaving only two choices: find shelter or flee. Cassidy Livingston's new identity has begun to feel as comfortable as her favorite sweater. She's been tucked away on Lantern Beach for weeks, waiting to testify against a deadly gang, and is settling in to a new life she wants to last forever. When she thinks she spots someone malevolent from her past, panic swells inside her. If an enemy has found her, Cassidy won't be the only one who's a target. Everyone she's come to love will also be at risk. Dangerous waters threaten to pull her into an overpowering chasm she may never escape. Can Cassidy survive what lies ahead? Or has the tide fatally turned against her?

Perilous Riptide

Just when the current seems safer, an unseen danger emerges and threatens to destroy everything. When Cassidy Livingston finds a journal hidden deep in the recesses of her ice cream truck, her curiosity kicks into high gear. Islanders suspect that Elsa, the journal's owner, didn't die accidentally. Her final entry indicates their suspicions might be correct and that what Elsa observed on her final night may have led to her demise. Against the advice of Ty Chambers, her former Navy SEAL boyfriend, Cassidy taps into her detective skills and hunts for answers. But her search only leads to a skeletal body and trouble for both of them. As helplessness threatens to drown her, Cassidy is desperate to turn back time. Can Cassidy find what she needs to navigate the perilous situation? Or will the riptide surrounding her threaten everyone and everything Cassidy loves?

Deadly Undertow

The current's fatal pull is powerful, but so is one detective's will to live. When someone from Cassidy Livingston's past shows up on Lantern Beach and warns her of impending peril, opposing currents collide, threatening to drag her under. Running would be easy. But leaving would break her heart. Cassidy must decipher between the truth and lies, between reality and deception. Even more importantly, she must decide whom to trust and whom to fear. Her life depends on it. As danger rises and answers surface, everything Cassidy thought she knew is tested. In order to survive, Cassidy must take drastic measures and end the battle against the ruthless gang DH-7 once and for all. But if her final mission fails, the consequences will be as deadly as the raging undertow.

LANTERN BEACH ROMANTIC SUSPENSE

Tides of Deception

Change has come to Lantern Beach: a new police chief, a new season, and . . . a new romance? Austin Brooks has loved Skye Lavinia from the moment they met, but the walls she keeps around her seem impenetrable. Skye knows Austin is the best thing to ever happen to her. Yet she also knows that if he learns the truth about her past, he'd be a fool not to run. A chance encounter brings secrets bubbling to the surface, and danger soon follows. Are the life-threatening events plaguing them really accidents . . . or is someone trying to send a deadly message? With the tides on Lantern Beach come deception and lies. One question remains—who will be swept away as the water shifts? And will it bring the end for Austin and Skye, or merely the beginning?

Shadow of Intrigue

For her entire life, Lisa Garth has felt like a supporting character in the drama of life. The designation never bothered her—until now. Lantern Beach, where she's settled and runs a popular restaurant, has boarded up for the season. The slower pace leaves her with too much time alone. Braden Dillinger came to Lantern Beach to try to heal. The former Special Forces officer returned from battle with invisible scars and diminished hope. But his recovery is hampered by the fact that an unknown enemy is trying to kill him. From the moment Lisa and Braden meet, danger ignites around them, and both are drawn into a web of intrigue that turns their lives upside down. As shadows creep in, will Lisa and Braden be able to shine a light on the peril around them? Or will the encroaching darkness turn their worst nightmares into reality?

Storm of Doubt

A pastor who's lost faith in God. A romance writer who's lost faith in love. A faceless man with a deadly obsession. Nothing has felt right in Pastor Jack Wilson's world since his wife died two years ago. He hoped coming to Lantern Beach might help soothe the ragged edges of his soul. Instead, he feels more alone than ever. Novelist Juliette Grace came to the island to hide away. Though her professional life has never been better, her personal life has imploded. Her husband left her and a stalker's threats have grown more and more dangerous. When Jack saves Juliette from an attack, he sees the terror in her gaze and knows he must protect her. But when danger strikes again, will Jack be able to keep her safe? Or will the approaching storm prove too strong to withstand?

Winds of Danger

Wes O'Neill is perfectly content to hang with his friends and enjoy island life on Lantern Beach.

Something begins to change inside him when Paige Henderson sweeps into his life. But the beautiful newcomer is hiding painful secrets beneath her cheerful facade. Police dispatcher Paige Henderson came to Lantern Beach riddled with guilt and uncertainties after the fallout of a bad relationship. When she meets Wes, she begins to open up to the possibility of love again. But there's something Wes isn't telling her—something that could change everything. As the winds shift, doubts seep into Paige's mind. Can Paige and Wes trust each other, even as the currents work against them? Or is trouble from the past too much to overcome?

Rains of Remorse

A stranger invades her home, leaving Rebecca Jarvis terrified. Above all, she must protect the baby growing inside her. Since her estranged husband died suspiciously six months earlier, Rebecca has been determined to depend on no one but herself. Her chivalrous new neighbor appears to be an answer to prayer. But who is Levi Stoneman really? Rebecca wants to believe he can help her, but she can't ignore her instincts. As danger closes in, both Rebecca and Levi must figure out whom they can trust. With Rebecca's baby coming soon, there's no time to waste. Can the truth prevail . . . or will remorse overpower the best of intentions?

LANTERN BEACH PD

On the Lookout

When Cassidy Chambers accepted the job as police chief on Lantern Beach, she knew the island had its secrets. But a suspicious death with potentially far-reaching implications will test all her skills —and threaten to reveal her true identity. Cassidy enlists the help of her husband, former Navy SEAL Ty Chambers. As they dig for answers, both uncover parts of their pasts that are best left buried. Not everything is as it seems, and they must figure out if their John Doe is connected to the secretive group that has moved onto the island. As facts materialize, danger on the island grows. Can Cassidy and Ty discover the truth about the shadowy crimes in their cozy community? Or has darkness permanently invaded their beloved Lantern Beach?

Attempt to Locate

A fun girls' night out turns into a nightmare when armed robbers barge into the store where Cassidy and her friends are shopping. As the situation escalates and the men escape, a massive manhunt launches on Lantern Beach to apprehend the dangerous trio. In the midst of the chaos, a potential foe asks for Cassidy's help. He needs to find his sister who fled from the secretive Gilead's Cove community on the island. But the more Cassidy learns about the seemingly untouchable group, the more her unease grows. The pressure to solve both cases continues to mount. But as the gravity of the situation rises, so does the danger. Cassidy is determined to protect the island and break up the cult . . . but doing so might cost her everything.

First Degree Murder

Police Chief Cassidy Chambers longs for a break from the recent crimes plaguing Lantern Beach. She simply wants to enjoy her friends' upcoming wedding, to prepare for the busy tourist season about to slam the island, and to gather all the dirt she can on the suspicious community that's invaded the town. But trouble explodes on the island, sending residents—including Cassidy—into a squall of uneasiness. Cassidy may have more than one enemy plotting her demise, and the collateral damage seems unthinkable. As the temperature rises, so does the pressure to find answers. Someone is determined that Lantern Beach would be better off without their new police chief. And for Cassidy, one wrong move could mean certain death.

Dead on Arrival

With a highly charged local election consuming the community, Police Chief Cassidy Chambers braces herself for a challenging day of breaking up petty conflicts and tamping down high emotions. But when widespread food poisoning spreads among potential voters across the island, Cassidy smells something rotten in the air. As Cassidy examines every possibility to uncover what's going on, local enigma Anthony Gilead again comes on her radar. The man is running for mayor and his cult-like following is growing at an alarming rate. Cassidy feels certain he has a spy embedded in her inner circle. The problem is that her pool of suspects gets deeper every day. Can Cassidy get to the bottom of what's eating away at her peaceful island home? Will voters turn out despite the outbreak of illness plaguing their tranquil town? And the even bigger question: Has darkness come to stay on Lantern Beach?

Plan of Action

A missing Navy SEAL. Danger at the boiling point. The ultimate showdown. When Police Chief Cassidy Chambers' husband, Ty, disappears, her world is turned upside down. His truck is discovered with blood inside, crashed in a ditch on Lantern Beach, but he's nowhere to be found. As they launch a manhunt to find him, Cassidy discovers that someone on the island has a deadly obsession with Ty. Meanwhile, Gilead's Cove seems to be imploding. As danger heightens, federal law enforcement officials are called in. The cult's growing threat could lead to the pinnacle standoff of good versus evil. A clear plan of action is needed or the results will be devastating. Will Cassidy find Ty in time, or will she face a gut-wrenching loss? Will Anthony Gilead finally be unmasked for who he really is and be brought to justice? Hundreds of innocent lives are at stake . . . and not everyone will come out alive.

THE WORST DETECTIVE EVER:

I'm not really a private detective. I just play one on TV.

Joey Darling, better known to the world as Raven Remington, detective extraordinaire, is trying to separate herself from her invincible alter ego. She played the spunky character for five years on the hit TV show *Relentless*, which catapulted her to fame and into the role of Hollywood's sweetheart. When her marriage falls apart, her finances dwindle to nothing, and her father disappears, Joey finds herself on the Outer Banks of North Carolina, trying to piece together her life away from the limelight. But as people continually mistake her for the character she played on TV, she's tasked with solving real life crimes . . . even though she's terrible at it.

COMPLETE BOOK LIST

Squeaky Clean Mysteries:

#13 Cold Case: Clean Getaway

#14 Cold Case: Clean Sweep

#15 Cold Case: Clean Break

#16 Cleans to an End (coming soon)

While You Were Sweeping, A Riley Thomas Spinoff

The Sierra Files:

#1 Pounced

#2 Hunted

#3 Pranced

#4 Rattled

The Gabby St. Claire Diaries (a Tween Mystery series):

The Curtain Call Caper

The Disappearing Dog Dilemma

The Bungled Bike Burglaries

The Worst Detective Ever

#1 Ready to Fumble

#2 Reign of Error

#3 Safety in Blunders

#4 Join the Flub

#5 Blooper Freak

#6 Flaw Abiding Citizen

#7 Gaffe Out Loud

#8 Joke and Dagger

#9 Wreck the Halls

#10 Glitch and Famous (coming soon)

Raven Remington

Relentless 1

Relentless 2 (coming soon)

Holly Anna Paladin Mysteries:

#1 Random Acts of Murder

#2 Random Acts of Deceit

#2.5 Random Acts of Scrooge

#3 Random Acts of Malice

#4 Random Acts of Greed

#5 Random Acts of Fraud

#6 Random Acts of Outrage

#7 Random Acts of Iniquity

Lantern Beach Mysteries

#1 Hidden Currents

#2 Flood Watch

#3 Storm Surge

#4 Dangerous Waters

#5 Perilous Riptide

#6 Deadly Undertow

Lantern Beach Romantic Suspense

Tides of Deception

Shadow of Intrigue

Storm of Doubt

Winds of Danger

Rains of Remorse

Lantern Beach P.D.

On the Lookout

Attempt to Locate

First Degree Murder

Dead on Arrival

Plan of Action

Lantern Beach Escape

Afterglow (a novelette)

Lantern Beach Blackout

Dark Water

Safe Harbor

Ripple Effect

Rising Tide

Crime á la Mode

Deadman's Float

Milkshake Up

Bomb Pop Threat (coming soon)

Banana Split Personalities (coming soon)

The Sidekick's Survival Guide

The Art of Eavesdropping

The Perks of Meddling

The Skill of Snooping (coming soon)

The Practice of Prying (coming soon)

Carolina Moon Series

Home Before Dark

Gone By Dark

Wait Until Dark

Light the Dark

Taken By Dark

Suburban Sleuth Mysteries:

Death of the Couch Potato's Wife

Fog Lake Suspense:

Edge of Peril

Margin of Error

Brink of Danger

Line of Duty

Cape Thomas Series:

Dubiosity

Disillusioned

Distorted

Standalone Romantic Mystery:

The Good Girl

Suspense:

Imperfect

The Wrecking

Sweet Christmas Novella:

Home to Chestnut Grove

Standalone Romantic-Suspense:

Keeping Guard

The Last Target

Race Against Time

Ricochet

Key Witness

Lifeline

High-Stakes Holiday Reunion

Desperate Measures

Hidden Agenda

Mountain Hideaway

Dark Harbor

Shadow of Suspicion

The Baby Assignment

The Cradle Conspiracy

Trained to Defend

Nonfiction:

Characters in the Kitchen

Changed: True Stories of Finding God through Christian Music (out of print)

The Novel in Me: The Beginner's Guide to Writing and Publishing a Novel (out of print)

ABOUT THE AUTHOR

USA Today has called Christy Barritt's books "scary, funny, passionate, and quirky."

Christy writes both mystery and romantic suspense novels that are clean with underlying messages of faith. Her books have won the Daphne du Maurier Award for Excellence in Suspense and Mystery, have been twice nominated for the Romantic Times Reviewers' Choice Award, and have finaled for both a Carol Award and Foreword Magazine's Book of the Year.

She is married to her Prince Charming, a man who thinks she's hilarious—but only when she's not trying to be. Christy is a self-proclaimed klutz, an avid music lover who's known for spontaneously bursting into song, and a road trip aficionado.

When she's not working or spending time with her family, she enjoys singing, playing the guitar, and exploring small, unsuspecting towns where people have no idea how accident-prone she is.

Find Christy online at:
www.christybarritt.com
www.facebook.com/christybarritt
www.twitter.com/cbarritt

Sign up for Christy's newsletter to get information on all of her latest releases here: www.christybarritt.com/newsletter-sign-up/

If you enjoyed this book, please consider leaving a review.

Made in United States
Orlando, FL
06 February 2024

43353472R00104